PUFFIN BOOKS

LOST IN TIME

Namita Gokhale is the author of twenty books, including eleven works of fiction. Namita's *The Puffin Mahabharata* is a classic retelling of the epic, a perennial favourite with readers young and old. She is the co-founder and co-director of the famous Jaipur Literature Festival and believes passionately in the power of stories and storytelling.

PRAISE FOR THE BOOK

'The book, apart from its engaging and succinct narrative, also holds your attention because of its illustrations. Beautiful monochrome sketches add to the story and make the journey a visual one, something that keeps you close to its characters and plot'—*Hindustan Times*

'Through lucid and easy English, the author has explained age-old secrets of the forest and the elemental forces for the book's young readers. To keep the interest and wonderment of children alive, the author writes about magic, teleporting, prescience and mind-boggling rakshasa technology that keep you in awe and thrall'—*Deccan Chronicle*

ALSO IN PUFFIN BY NAMITA GOKHALE

The Puffin Mahabharata

LOST IN TIME

*Ghatotkacha and the
Game of Illusions*

NAMITA GOKHALE

Illustrations by Ujan Dutta

PUFFIN BOOKS
An imprint of Penguin Random House

PUFFIN BOOKS

USA | Canada | UK | Ireland | Australia
New Zealand | India | South Africa | China

Puffin Books is part of the Penguin Random House group of companies
whose addresses can be found at global.penguinrandomhouse.com

Published by Penguin Random House India Pvt. Ltd
4th Floor, Capital Tower 1, MG Road,
Gurugram 122 002, Haryana, India

Penguin
Random House
India

First published in Puffin Books by Penguin Random House India 2017
This edition published in Puffin Books by Penguin Random House India 2022

ISBN 9780143334187

For sale in the Indian subcontinent only

Typeset in Adobe Caslon Pro by Manipal Digital Systems, Manipal

www.penguin.co.in

This book is dedicated to my readers, young and old, especially all those who read and reread The Puffin Mahabharata.

To the great Indian epics, and the culture that visualized them.

To all the schoolchildren, brimming with ideas and intelligence, who have inspired me over the years, especially my young friends at Vasant Valley School.

To Raemona Rashna Panda for the wonderful title suggestion.

To my granddaughters, Anina and Anisha, and my grandson Krishna, and their love of books.

To the child in all of us.

Contents

To Return to the Beginning

I am Chintamani Dev Gupta, male, 4'11", thirteen years of age. Almost fourteen. It won't surprise anyone to know that my name was, at an early and vulnerable age, shortened to Chintu, then mutated to Chintu Pintu. It's ignominy to have a name like Chintu Pintu, but it's a cross I've learnt to bear. I feel like telling them—the sneerers—'Man, you don't know where I've been, you don't know what I've seen!'

The story that will unfold in these pages has been recorded with all the memory megabytes at my disposal, but when you—they—I—travel through time, *across* time, the grey cells tend to seize up and short-circuit in transit.

But let me begin at the beginning. If there ever is a beginning, if time follows a straight line, follows a predictable geometric pattern in its unfolding. Which I happen to know, from my incredible personal experiences, it does not.

Those of you (possibly in the minority) who have read Carl Sagan's book *Contact* might appreciate wormholes and the ways to fool or get fooled by time. Whereas those of you who are fans of Terry Pratchett (more hands up this time maybe) might remember that he said, 'Stories of imagination tend to upset those without one.'

But I've nattered on enough. Let's get to the flashback with Chintamani Dev Gupta (aka Chintu Pintu) off on an enforced holiday to Sat Tal Birding Camp. I remember it as though it were yesterday. My parents had just split up, even though they continued to be holed up in the same house. Mum's lady lawyer practically camped on our living room sofa. Papa hadn't shaved for several days. Things were bad. And to get me out of the way, I had been dispatched here, to an insect-infested field near the aforementioned Sat Tal Lake.

It's not like I was wildly interested in birds. I suspect it was just the most convenient way to pack me off, dumping me in ornithology heaven. So there I was, amidst the tweets and the cheeps and the trills and twitters of birdsong, dreaming of football and butter chicken and the joys of home.

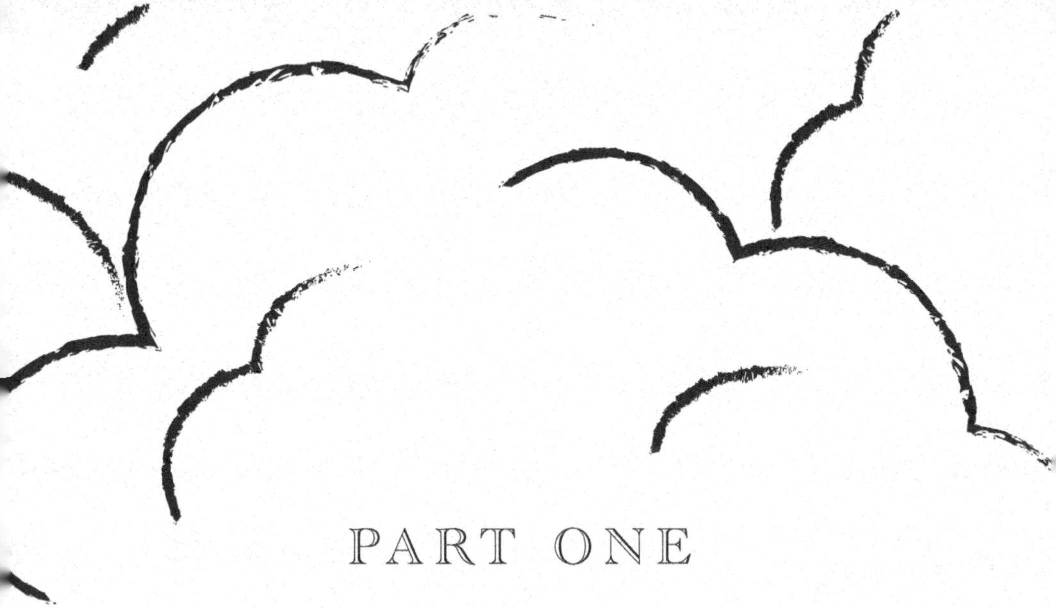

PART ONE

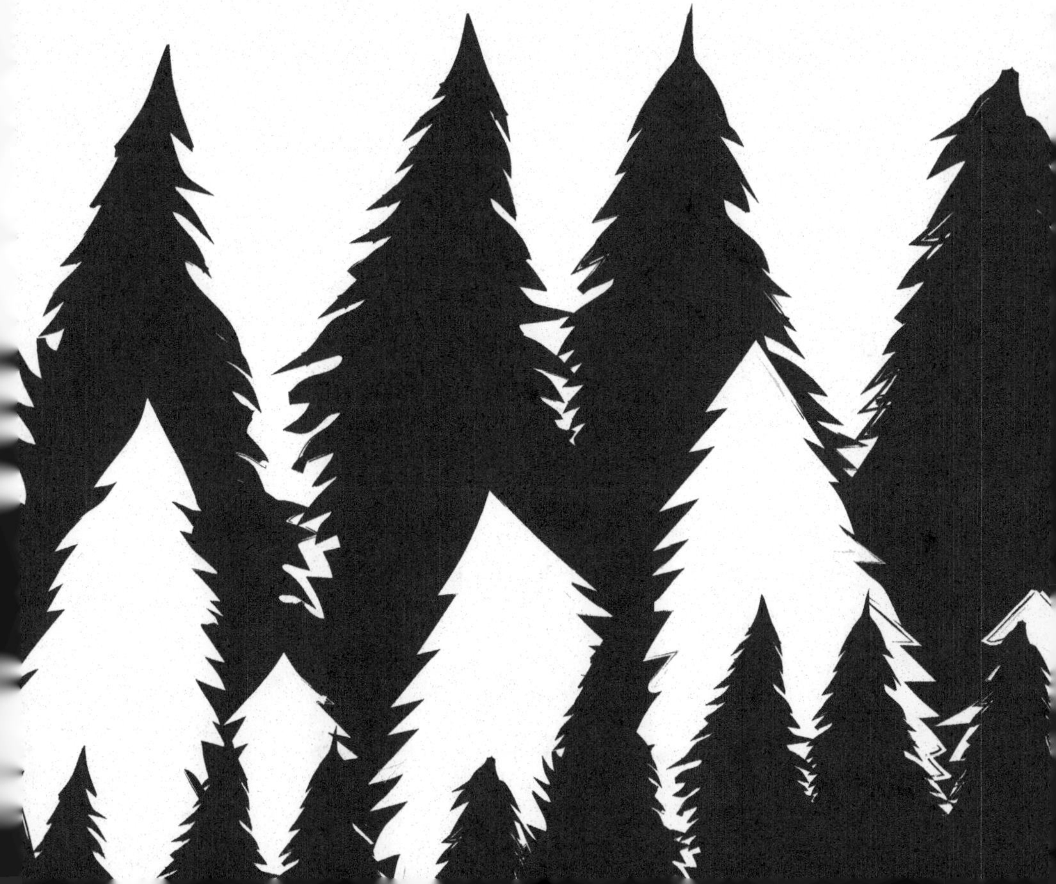

A Trek through Time

It was a really hot day. I slowly slid into the cool waters of the lake, as peaceable as a baby in a bathtub. I hadn't told the group master, Mr Sushil, that I was planning a swim. He wouldn't have allowed it. It was more like a military camp than a birdwatchers' group. We had been divided into 'houses', and I was in Bulbul. There were some nice kids in Magpie, Hoopoe sounded fun by name and then there was Monal. I had deserted all the dull Bulbul kids and gone off for a solitary swim, just to be alone with my thoughts for a bit, with my worries and anxieties about the exploding nest back in Gurgaon.

The sky was a deep, piercing blue. The water was green, with a blue underside to the gentle waves. I switched from my usual steady breaststroke to a languid backstroke. A small, friendly-looking cloud, shaped uncannily like a duck, floated in the sky above.

It took me a little time to realize that something was wrong. The sky was looking hazier, and my body was suddenly feeling heavier—THUD! My head had hit against something. I still don't know what that something was, but I saw stars—a whole crazy constellation of them—buzzing around my head. My life started flashing before me, all thirteen years of it, in furiously

accelerated motion . . . things I had forgotten, things I couldn't ever remember remembering.

I was being sucked into the water, deeper and deeper, in a sort of whirlpool. But I wasn't drowning. I was, in fact, breathing quite normally, considering the state I was in, just panting and gasping and wishing madly that I was home with my mum in Gurgaon. *Perhaps the lake is highly oxygenated*, I told myself, trying to stay rational, *or maybe heaven is a sky full of H2O?*

The water was clear almost all the way to the bottom. Huge boulders sat on the bed of the lake, covered with dull-green slime, looking like enormous overstuffed velvet sofa sets. I tried desperately to resist, to rise up and surface, but it was as though some determined magnetic force was steering me. I discovered I was in a vortex of whirling waves but, incredibly, still quite dry, as if I had been packaged in some sort of invisible waterproofing. Then, without warning, I was sucked into the sofa-like rocks, and everything went dark.

My ears felt strange—like they do when a plane is about to land—and there was a sort of decompression and then I was a sack of potatoes hurled into an endless pit. This went on for a very long, or very short, time; I really couldn't figure out which. It wasn't dark any more, though. A sort of dappled light filtered down to wherever I was, as if I was surrounded by bubble wrap. It was also glacially cold, and I felt chilled and numbed and incoherently afraid.

Then I was on the shore, walking on a patch of pebble and sand. I was still wearing my swimming trunks and my waterproof swim watch. But everything around me was quite different from when I had stepped into the waters. The colour of the sky was different. It had a tinge of purple in it, something I had never known or noticed before. The air felt different, thinner and sharper than usual. There was a strange smell in the air too, as though I had wandered into the zoo by accident. And the line of dhabas by the steps leading to the lake, selling kadhi chawal and rajma chawal and iced Frooti, had disappeared altogether from any line of vision, like they had never existed at all.

I pinched myself, hard, to check if I was still alive, if I still existed. *Where are you, Chintu Pintu?* I asked myself, *and what the ***** **** is happening?* I don't normally use swear words; they seem unnecessary. But they seemed necessary then, in that moment. I blinked and, scratching my head, looked at the lake, hoping this was a momentary hallucination and things might just revert to normal. I would have given my life for the sight of Mr Sushil walking towards me down the shore.

Instead I saw a creature—no other word for it—in the water, with a long, snake-like head and diamond-shaped scaly green fins. It looked faintly bored, and its beady eyes observed me with a sort of vague, speculative interest. This was not a crocodile or a plastic boat, and in any case, Sat Tal Lake had neither. This was a plesiosaur if I ever saw one . . . or a pliosaur . . . or some such ancient Loch Ness monster. It didn't matter which; I ran for dear life!

Someone—something—was scampering alongside in the springy grass. As I stopped to get my bearings, it raced ahead of me—a large

rabbit with improbably long ears. It halted for a moment and turned to look back. On its face was a goofy lopsided grin, and I suddenly felt reassured. This was a dream . . . a dream, *not* a nightmare, and the monster in the lake was just a graphic pop-up figment of my unconscious, or an abandoned inflatable toy . . .

The rabbit was still examining me with more than normal curiosity, as if I, Chintamani, in my faded swimming trunks and waterproof watch, was a creature from some new and fantastical world altogether. Suddenly it pricked up its ears and raised its tail, listening intently to some unheard sound, before bounding off into the shadows.

It was getting dark. The sky was rapidly changing colour from pink to purple, and a gleaming sickle moon soon appeared, imperceptibly gliding into view from behind a tree. Venus glittered beside it, brighter than any diamond I had ever seen, as though it had been digitally enhanced. It flashed and throbbed like a pinpoint of white fire, outshining any stellar body I had ever imagined. What was going on here?

I sat down on the grass and stared some more at the heavens. It was like a theatre gently dimming, and then suddenly the show began. The stars leapt to life, one by one at first and then in rapid clumps of dancing, spinning light. There were thousands and thousands of them! So many that I couldn't relate them to any sky map or nightscape I had ever encountered. Some of them were bright and steady, others twinkled and whirled in different shades and spectrums, almost as if they were speaking to me. Try as I might, I couldn't make out the constellations; the red star surely wasn't Mars, and which was the one pulsating with the blue light?

I guess Gurgaon has pretty much shut out the night, except as a biological habit . . . but there, then, I felt like I was falling into the sky, swimming in it, drowning in it. There went a shooting star, and then another. I made two wishes:

1. I wanted my parents to be happy, and together, as they used to be.
2. I wanted to be a football star. A tall football star.

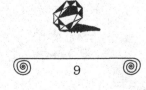

A figure was approaching. He, she, it, was holding a burning branch of wood and breathing deeply. I had slouched down, suddenly tired and drowsy, in a bed of dry leaves. An enormous face came into view a long way above me. I wondered if I was dreaming, but the warmth from the flaming torch seeped into my bones, as did the long, careful breaths of this giant. I sat up bolt upright.

He was sniffing me, and I could smell him too. The tang of leaves and the forest, with a whiff of animal and the scent of human.

'Who are you?' he asked in a language I didn't understand. And yet, strangely enough, I did. Was this telepathy?

'And who are you?!' I asked back, the question put forward in sheer panic mixed with some cunning. I was still trying to take in the awesome size of this Godzilla, and figured my question might help establish a bond with this primeval creature. But then, how would he understand my question, which probably sounded more like a squeal?

'I am Ghatotkacha,' he replied. 'I am the rakshasa Ghatotkacha, born of the lord Bhimasena and the lady Hidimbi. I rule over hill and vale, jungle and stream, to protect the spirit of the forest and all who live in it.'

I understood this too, through some sort of teleprompter that seemed to have lodged itself somewhere in the left lobe of my brain like a Google Translate implant.

'I am Chintamani Dev Gupta,' I replied tentatively. But it wasn't *me* speaking at all, perhaps some sort of decoder that seemed to be picking up on signals from my brain. *Take control*, I told myself, *take control, or you will lose this mind game.*

'I am speaking Paisachi, but I am fluent in Prakrit and Sanskrit too,' the giant replied.

He had huge red eyes that were lit up by the burning torch he held in his hand. But they were kind eyes . . . there was not even a hint of cruelty in them.

'And don't worry, I am not trying to take control of your mind!'

Weird, weirder, weirdest. He could actually read my mind! Holy cow! This situation was just impossible. I pinched myself even harder this time, so that I might now wake up from this fast-accelerating nightmare.

'Yes, I too respect the holy cows! My father is a Kshatriya and in honour of his dharma, I protect the kin and cattle of the learned Brahmans in the nearby villages,' he replied in response to my unspoken exclamation.

'I-I-I'm hungry, and tired, and afraid . . .' I whimpered. It seemed like a good idea to speak the truth and nothing but the truth to this magical mind reader.

But still, I was watching my thoughts. Ghatotkacha didn't reply. Wordlessly, he scooped me up in his massive arms and we took off, flying through the sky above the treetops. The wind was whistling through my ears. Though fatigue had gripped my body, my head reeled. This was insane!

The sky above us was aflame with stars, getting dark again as we began descending to earth and were enveloped by the stillness of the sleeping forest. There was a clearing by a stream that was lit up by the unnaturally bright moonlight and the glow of a few scattered torches. I could see the rushing silver waves and hear the swift rhythm of the water too clearly. The scene was something out of a movie.

'Ghatto'—as I had sleepily decided to call him—flew me down to the clearing. There was a dwelling there, a sort of hut made of a circle of tall trees. *Sal trees*, my internal voices prompted. A woman stood by the doorway. She was taller than Ghatto, and wearing nothing save a bark skirt. A necklace of skulls almost reached her knees.

'He is hungry! This little baby is hungry!'

She spoke in what I now recognized as Paisachi. As had happened with Ghatto, I could decrypt what she was saying somewhere in the left lobe of my brain.

'The little puppy is hungrrry!' she went on in cute, lisping monster baby talk, as though I were a pet. Well, of course I *was* little compared to their freaking outsize bodies. And I was, as she had said, indeed very hungry.

'This is Hidimbi Ma,' Ghatto explained. 'My mother, wife of the mighty warrior Bhimasena, eldest daughter-in-law of Queen Kunti.' He did not introduce me to her.

We entered the dwelling. It was pitch-dark inside, with no moonlight and no torches either for illumination.

'We rakshasas can see best in the dark,' Ghatto explained further, 'but I will summon some light for you.'

I looked up in utter astonishment to see that the circle of sal trees had a roof of entwined creepers. This roof was now lit up with festoons of blinking green lights. From the centre unravelled a dangling forest chandelier of leaves and fireflies. It was all so unexpected that it took my breath away. I was no longer tired or hungry or afraid, but simply lost in the wonder of this waking dream.

A gleaming brass cauldron appeared in the centre of the tree-room and a fire spontaneously blazed up at the base. Then an enormous boar's head surfaced in the cauldron and started to merrily bubble away in a stew of red berries.

'My favourite dish in all the world!' Ghatto whispered to me. And I had to agree, it smelled divine.

Before long, it was ready. They just dug into the food, mother and son, with their long claw-like nails. I noticed that Hidimbi Ma's curling, pointy ones were lacquered a bright-red colour, as though she had used nail polish. My mother used that very shade sometimes. However, I stood by the edge of the cauldron and sniffed at it wistfully. I had to stand on tiptoe to peep in. How was I to eat this?

Hidimbi Ma had read my mind. A table and a chair appeared at the speed of light. A green plastic bowl materialized next, with a generous helping of the boar soup. A green plastic spoon, fork and knife were also magically laid out on the table, along with, inexplicably, a neatly folded polka-dotted paper napkin! I wolfed down my meal and fell asleep then and there, on the wooden table, with my head slumped against the empty bowl. Was it my imagination, or did it have a Chhota Bheem logo on it?

I have a faint memory of being carried up and floating through the air in Hidimbi Ma's arms. She smelled comforting, and familiar. The fragrance of green leaves and crushed flowers was about her—I could picture her having played in the forest all day long. It was probably just the shampoo she used.

The Master of Illusions

I slept in a cosy cubbyhole, nested like a birdhouse high up in one of the tall tree-walls of the rakshasa's house. When I awoke I found that I was no longer in my rather inadequate swimming-trunks-and-waterproof-watch combo, but in my favourite checked night suit. Rays of bright sunshine peeped in through the leaves and creepers. *This was not a dream*, I told myself. It was lasting far too long to be one. In the morning light, my surroundings felt real—the gnarled texture of the bark walls, the ladybird crawling up the tangled vines, the blue of the sky that I could glimpse between the curtains of glossy green foliage. I was resigning myself to the strangeness of it all—it was quite beyond me to decipher where I was and why. As I was figuring out how to make my way down, a rope ladder unfolded in obedience to my unvoiced anxiety.

Ghatotkacha was in the clearing outside the house, looking distinctly preoccupied. I noticed he had enormous jug-shaped ears, curly hair like the Amazon Jungle and skin the colour of a copper coin. He smiled when he saw me, but I could see that his mind was on other things. He was counting on his long fingers and muttering things in a language I couldn't understand, even though he was counting out loud. I realized that this was because he was speaking to himself—he wasn't trying to communicate with me. Curiouser and curiouser.

Then he spoke to me. This time it appeared to me as something between a thought bubble and a comic-strip speech balloon. 'What would you like to eat?' he asked.

I was touched, and impressed. For someone who was clearly in the middle of figuring out a problem, here he was bothering to find out if I was hungry!

What *did* I want for breakfast? Before I could think about it, a platter of fruits materialized, floating above an upended tree trunk like a strange butterfly. Bananas and a fleshy fruit that looked somewhat like the hairy durians we had enjoyed on our family holiday in Singapore last year. It had been the last 'family' thing in a long time. I wondered about my parents—how they were, how much they were worrying about me.

Then it struck me! If I asked for a mobile phone, with all the telepathic wish-granting that was going on, I would get one!

'I want a phone!' I cried out. 'An iPhone? . . . Or even my old cracked-screen Samsung. Oh, and connectivity—I need good network!'

Ghatotkacha looked faintly annoyed. His eyebrows, each the size of the largish bananas that had appeared before me, furrowed and crinkled.

'I can't get you a phone,' he responded, the reply hanging between speech and the left-brain teleprompting that had become our established way of talking.

'But why not? Why *can't* you get me an iPhone if you can get me polka-dotted paper napkins and all that crap?' I replied, rather petulantly I suppose. But the enormous giant before me was grinning good-naturedly. I had amused rather than irritated him.

Then he stood up to his full height, towering above me like the Qutub Minar. 'I am Ghatotkacha, the master of illusions!' he proclaimed. 'The rakshasa race understands the nature of illusions. We know how to make night into day—and day into night. It is a game we play with the shadows of the mind and the powers of the elements.'

Even as he said this, the sky darkened and I could see the stars light up above me.

'We know how to play with perception,' he continued, his voice sounding very serious indeed in the dark. 'And as for the truth . . . no one in the three worlds knows what the truth is. But *technology*,' he used the word cautiously, as though he were testing it, 'communication technology, is a good, collaborative phenomenon. We can probe your world, and with the gift my great-grandmother, Trikaalini, bequeathed me, I can break the veil of time and see into other ages. But I cannot resurrect an entire beehive of perception, not even with my powers of illusion . . .'

The sky was not dark any more, and suddenly there was a phone in my hand, an Apple iPhone 5—but I could see it was just a toy. It didn't even have the right markings, or a battery. My mind was reeling. Ghatotkacha did make everything sound reasonable and logical . . . but WTF was happening?

Sometimes in a dream, you know, or suspect, that you are dreaming. That's what I felt like, but the opposite—this was not lucid dreaming or a hallucination, even though it was surely unreal.

My mother is a translator. She spends her time before a computer and in a sea of books. And dictionaries. French. Spanish. Hindi. Behind her desk is a framed quotation, which she'd printed out from somewhere. It says, 'The translator may be the one person who exists simultaneously in two different worlds.'

'Correction!' I wanted to tell her as I sat contemplating the strangeness of the situation that afternoon. 'Translators are NOT the only ones; time travellers do too! My situation now, bro!'

Instead I asked the giant curiously, 'When exactly in history do you live, Ghatotkacha?' It was important to get my bearings.

'This is the end of the Dwapara yuga,' he replied. 'It is the age of Lord Krishna and his brother Balarama; of my family, the Pandavas; their cousins, the Kauravas; of Shantanu, Bhima, Drona, Karna, Draupadi and Abhimanyu. The Kali yuga, the time of trouble and decline, will follow soon. I suspect you are from that same Kali yuga, but quite some time ahead in the future.'

I let out a long whistle of total appreciation. This was crazy. I knew of the Mahabharata and all that stuff, but that I may be *in* it was *completely* insane. 'My father—he's called Abhimanyu!' I responded excitedly. 'But you're one of the Pandavas? Huh! Never heard of you somehow.'

But he wasn't paying attention to my enthusiasm. His large jug-like ears were flapping in a most disconcerting way.

'Do that again,' he said. 'That sound you just made . . .'

So I whistled again, and the note rang out strong and melodious in that quiet clearing in the forest.

'Again, please,' Ghatotkacha asked, and I obliged.

'Teach me.' It was between a request and a command.

I tried to show him how to contract his lips and blow out through his tongue. He peered into my mouth to understand better. What a large face he had! But it was a kind face, and so I trusted him. I was not afraid.

Finally, he let out a high-pitched warbling whistle and looked delighted. With himself, and with me. A quick learner.

'Abhimanyu is my cousin,' he continued, 'and I have just received a message from him. I was thinking of that when you arrived . . .' Then he whistled again, a long, happy, triumphant whistle. 'Hah! I think I have just found the solution to his problem. Let's go-oo-oo!'

And once again I found myself flying through the air with Ghatotkacha. Seriously, what was with him? Flying off here, there and everywhere without even a flipping wing in sight!

I watched the lands below. When we fly in our time, on our planes, we see roads and cities and snatches of nature before landing, but here, below us, were rivers and forests uninterrupted by human habitation.

'We are going to Dwarka to avenge the honour of my brother Abhimanyu,' Ghatotkacha informed me.

'I know Dwarka,' I was about to say; I realized just in time that it was the ancient city he was talking about, not the Delhi Dwarka where my maths tutor lives.

'The drowned city of Dwarka!' I replied excitedly, feeling like I had pressed the right button at the very last minute during a TV quiz. 'They discovered it recently.'

Ghatotkacha ignored me. 'Let me update you,' he said. 'Recently, I met my cousin Abhimanyu in the nearby forest. We did not know each other then, and battled almost to our deaths— until Mother Hidimbi and Aunt Subhadra understood that we both belong to the Pandava clan.

'Abhimanyu was on his way to Dwarka as my father and uncles are in exile, having lost their kingdom in a game of dice.

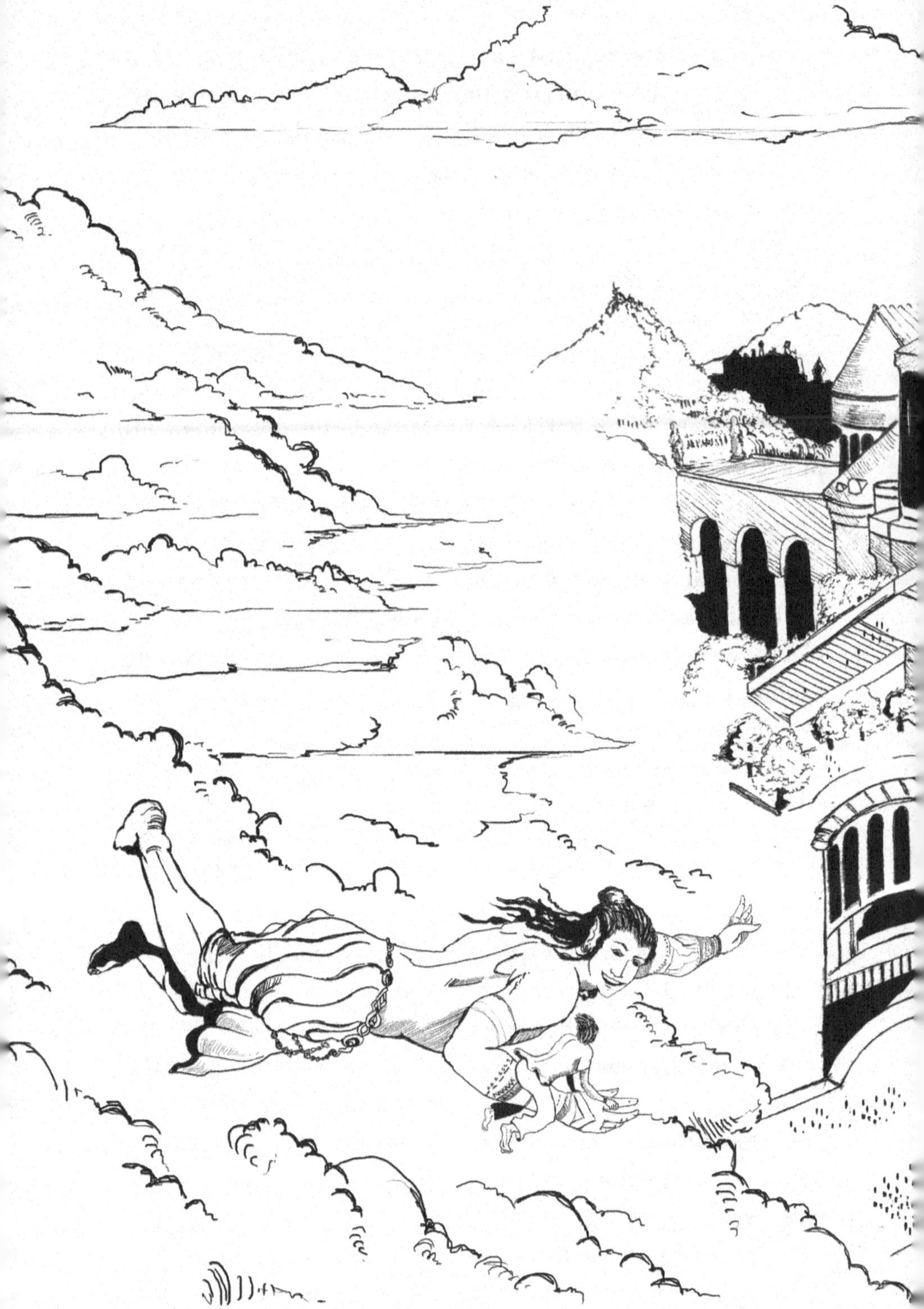

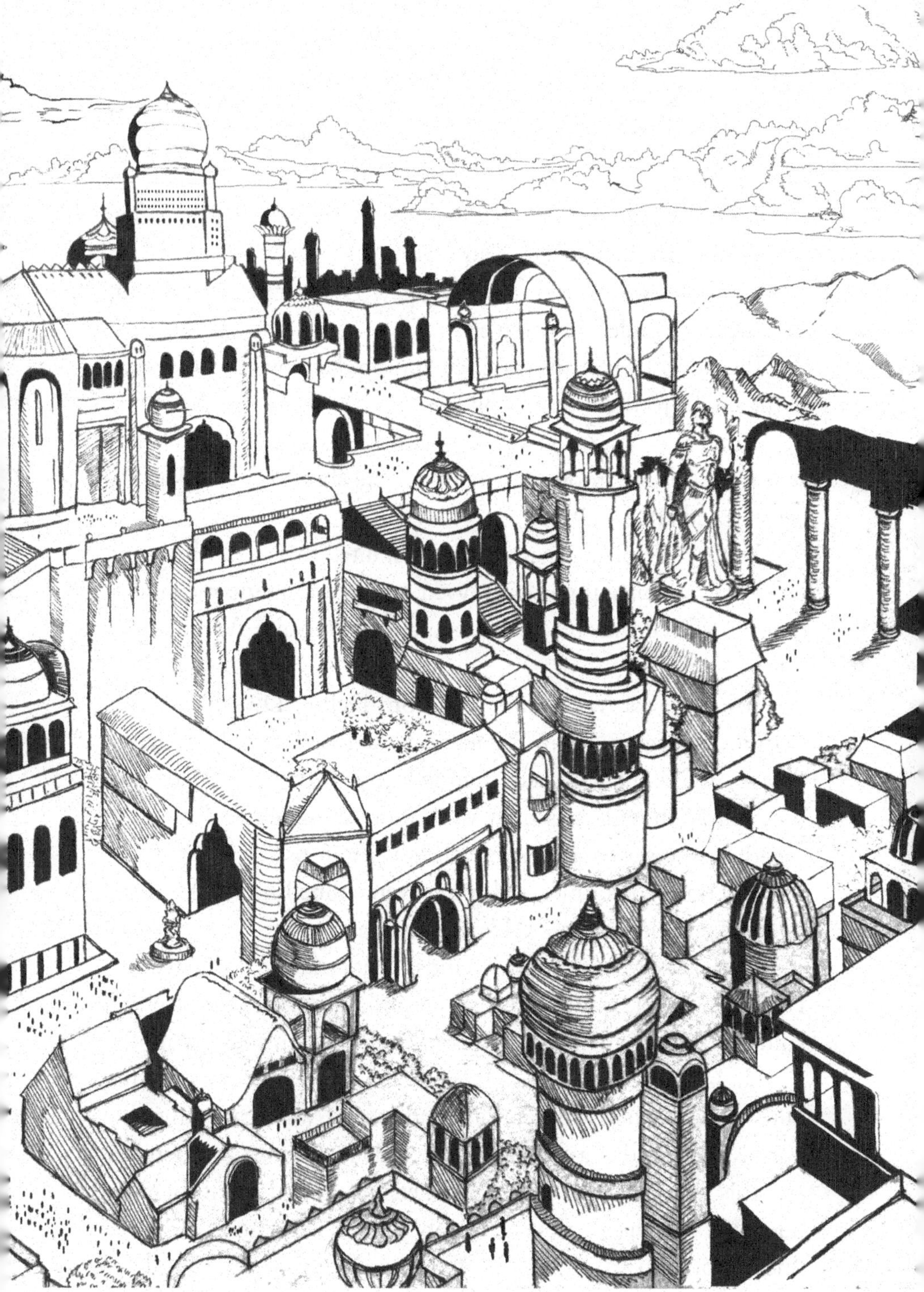

Abhimanyu was to be married to Vatsala, daughter of Lord Balarama, but her father, the king, has gone back on his word! My handsome cousin loves Vatsala, but she will be married soon to Prince Lakshmana of the Kauravas, who is the son of Lord Duryodhana.'

Honestly, it sounded like a B-grade mythological film. What was I doing in the middle of all this?

'And I—we—have to avenge Abhimanyu's honour,' Ghatotkacha ended impassively.

The silver spires of Dwarka appeared below us. We were flying closer to the ground now.

'Time to swing into action,' Ghatotkacha said. 'I have already sent my rakshasa troops to buy up all the shops in Dwarka! The eight-gated city awaits us.'

'What's the plan, Ghatotkacha?' I wanted to ask, but he began whistling, a jaunty tune that revved me up and made me believe that we—Ghatotkacha and I—could really retrieve Abhimanyu's honour! Way to go!

This Dwarka was as different from Delhi's Dwarka as Paris is from Paharganj. From my aerial view I had already gathered that it was a meticulously planned city, with wide roads and boulevards, though bits of it were more cramped and huddled together. The same large stone slabs were in use in most of the construction. The domes and spires were embellished with silver, and with shining diamond cones and squares.

'They are crystals, not diamonds,' Ghatotkacha corrected me. He had, as ever, astutely read my mind. 'Hold on now, we will land soon, and I am going to gear us both into invisibility mode.'

Ha ha ha! *Gear us into invisibility mode!* Ghatto was getting quite cool with his conversation! And indeed, we became invisible even as we landed in a crowded quadrangle with shops all around us.

This was a bustling clothes market, and rich garments of every hue and fabric hung around us: robes and scarves and turbans of fine cotton and splendid silk. A town crier sat in the middle of the square, alternating between blowing a trilling instrument, a kind of bugle, and excitedly uttering an announcement. I couldn't understand what he was saying, but Ghatotkacha telepathically whispered a translation to me.

'Hear ye, hear ye!' he was saying. 'New clothes for old! A magical bargain! New clothes for old! Hear ye! Hear ye!'

I could see that we truly were invisible, for people were pushing and jostling all around us. They looked puzzled when they bumped into our unseen bodies, then resumed their mad stampede towards the shops. It was like an H&M sale I had once been to with my mother in one of the big malls.

We were inside one of the stores now, where a supernaturally calm salesperson was swiftly exchanging old garments for the new ones he was handing out in their stead.

'He is one of us,' Ghatotkacha informed me. 'A rakshasa, in the guise of a human. You can always tell by the ears.' I looked at his ears, partially hidden by sidelocks and a yellow turban. They were a little longer than normal, and the skin was curiously crinkled.

'Ears are the hardest to transfigure during a metamorphosis,' Ghatto continued. 'They are external organs, and we have to work hard at getting them right.'

'But why are you doing this?' I asked, then gave up. Nothing around me made a shard of sense, and it was a waste of time to try to understand any of it.

'Well, the customers who are looking for this magical exchange are all Duryodhana's men,' Ghatotkacha explained. 'They are from the bridal party of Lakshmana, his son, who has arrived in Dwarka to marry Vatsala. Just watch this story unfold!'

And then, in the twinkling of an eye, I found myself in the most beautiful palace I had ever seen. Not that I have seen many palaces, only those in books and films and video games and on television. And Red Fort in Delhi and Amer Fort in Rajasthan.

But *this* was a *real* palace. It glittered and shimmered all around. And the stonework was strategically embedded with silver grills encrusted with emeralds and crystals. We were still invisible and in a luxurious room, which overlooked a calm ocean. Palm fronds framed a large picture window. A magnificent cockatoo examined us from an enormous elaborate cage, as though it could sense if not see us. A sad-eyed girl robed all in green was staring out at the sea. She didn't see us come in, of course.

However, within moments, Ghatotkacha had transformed into human shape; he was now dressed like the man in the bazaar and wore a pale-brown turban with gold edging. I thought he looked quite handsome as I watched out for his ears. And yes, they looked somehow odd—and crinkled! I too had transformed into a young courtier; there was even a golden ring on my right pinkie. From the little roll of cloth dangling down my shoulder, I surmised that my turban was a bright parrot green. Not my favourite colour, but there was little I could do about it.

My companion coughed respectfully and the girl turned to him in surprise. She had the longest hair, braided with flowers; it reached all the way to her knees.

'I am Ghatotkacha, son of Bhimasena, cousin to the royal Abhimanyu. I bring you his letter, where he pleads with you to travel with me to meet him. He is waiting with his mother, Subhadra, in the forest near Varanvata. He loves you, and wants to marry you.' He handed her a piece of bark marked with deep-violet ink.

I don't know what happened to me at that point in time . . . but I got a sudden and overpowering craving for pizza! Maybe it was a sort of displaced homesickness, but the imagined smell of cheese and pepperoni and a crisp base hit me like a physical blow. Ghatotkacha looked at me concernedly but didn't say anything.

'Sister Vatsala, will you come with me?' he asked.

She nodded wordlessly, and before I knew it, we were off in the air again, amidst the fleecy clouds, with the silver domes of Dwarka receding behind us. But this time, we were flying in a chariot, the Pushpaka Vimana, which is commonplace in the pages of an Amar Chitra Katha comic book. I supposed he couldn't have carried the both of us in his arms, and she might not have enjoyed the ride anyway.

We whizzed through the clouds, and before long, we were in a pretty hermitage in the same sort of landscape as Ghatotkacha's home, but what was clearly a human habitation. Abhimanyu and his mother, Subhadra, stood waiting for us. Abhimanyu was an incredibly good-looking young man, with an aquiline nose and a firm jawline and the fullest abs I have ever seen. Vatsala's eyes lit up when she saw him, and she bent down to touch Mother Subhadra's feet. An aged rishi with a long white beard tottered in, and she touched his feet too. But before I could watch the

scene unravel further, I was whisked away in Ghatotkacha's arms again. The Pushpaka Vimana had inexplicably disappeared, dematerialized into thin air.

We stopped at a clearing a little way away, where—would you believe it?—I found a piping hot pizza awaiting me! I ate it up ravenously and, with the last slice in my hand, we were off again. I discovered I was no longer feeling homesick or nostalgic about my long-ago days-of-future-past life. In fact, I felt strangely elated. I had completely surrendered to the present flow of events in this unexpected new time and place; I had a slice of pepperoni pizza in my hands and the wind in my hair. Could it get any better?

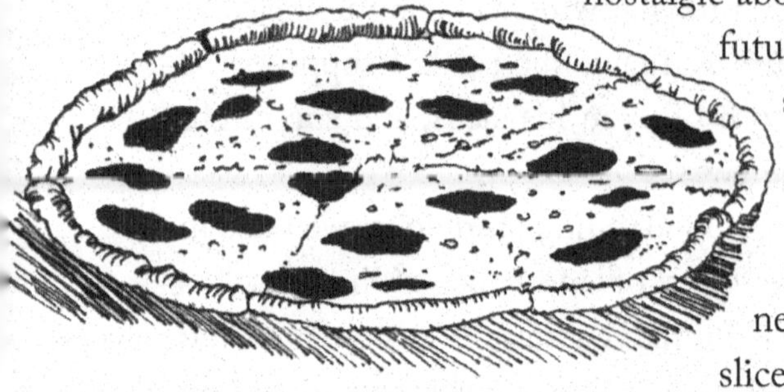

'Speed! We need speed!' Ghatotkacha muttered under his breath. In what seemed like seconds, we were back in Dwarka; the silver domes and spires seemed almost as familiar as Gurgaon by now.

Invisible again, we arrived at Princess Vatsala's bedchamber. The cockatoo in its ornate silver cage let out a long, low whistle, as if in greeting. Ghatotkacha responded with an upbeat version of the same tune—a mellow, deep first note followed by an excitable, shrill chirp.

I was getting used to being invisible; it's no big deal, really—just like some standard stealth mode technology. It's to do with bending light and the electromagnetic spectrum; but it doesn't feel all that different inside you.

All this casual nonchalance turned to shock, though, when I observed my rakshasa friend transform from being invisible to his old, rather frightening form and then into the beauteous Vatsala herself! The ears were a giveaway, as always, but otherwise, it was Princess Vatsala in the flesh.

'Is that really you, Ghatto?' I asked timidly. Nothing was as it seemed. I noticed that the waves outside too had changed; they were not as calm as they had been. They were ruffled and angry now, beating against the shore in an insistent sort of way.

'Yes, it's me,' he replied in his gruff rakshasa manner, before switching to a sweet ladylike voice that sounded like the strumming of a sarod—honestly!

'You stay invisible and close to me, Chintu Pintu,' Vatsala continued. 'There's a bit of excitement ahead!'

Chintu Pintu? I had never told him about the nickname that had tormented my childhood!

'Come along, young un,' he said in his rakshasa voice again. 'The wedding bells are pealing.'

Indeed there were bugles and drums and brass bells and the excited chatter of voices to be heard. An elderly lady entered, accompanied by a group of young women, all dressed to the nines.

They escorted 'Vatsala' and my invisible self down a steep flight of steps. The cockatoo whistled after us, then said, 'Come along, young un!' in Ghatotkacha's voice. Clever cockatoo! But nobody noticed, and there we were in the great hall, where King Balarama and his wife awaited the union of their daughter and her bridegroom.

Lord Duryodhana, a proud figure of a man, stood beside his son Prince Lakshmana. Duryodhana looked arrogant yet incredibly charming . . . like Rajinikanth, if you know what I mean. The Kauravas were there too, all hundred of them, with their courtiers and hangers-on.

I was watching it all intently, holding my breath at the magnificence around me. I could smell the marigolds and the lotus buds that had been strung all around. The priests began blowing their conch shells and a mighty wail echoed through the hall. Then a tall, commanding-looking man recited some verses in Sanskrit and handed a garland of white-and-red flowers strung with crystals to Lakshmana. I guessed he planned to put this around the bowed head of his shy-looking bride-to-be, the pretty princess Vatsala. But this was not to be.

The 'princess' gave Prince Lakshmana a demure smile, then pretended she was feeling dizzy. She clutched at his hand to steady herself. She held it tight, then tighter, with her mighty rakshasa strength.

Lakshmana winced, then staggered. He had gone pale with the pressure of those tender hands, and now he fell down in a dead faint by my feet. I saw it, I was there, though invisible.

As King Balarama, his queen, the guests—all were staring at him in surprise and consternation, I was promptly lifted up in Vatsala's—Ghatotkacha's—arms, and before anybody could understand what was happening, we were flying away together. Soon an army of rakshasas was following us, the 'shopkeepers' who had exchanged 'old clothes for new'. They looked gleeful, like children on a picnic, giggling and guffawing. Fine silken garments flew like ships in sail behind them—robes, scarves, turbans in every possible hue.

'My rakshasa troops sure tricked these city folks!' Ghatto giggled. 'They have been left disrobed and naked and feeling like fools! Hah! They were magical clothes—the magic can't be sustained once my armies have left, so the clothes are following us. The Kauravas,' his voice went hard, 'the despicable Kauravas, who sought to humiliate my cousin Abhimanyu, are themselves humiliated and the laughing stock of Dwarka!'

'What happens next?' I asked.

'*What happens next?* Abhimanyu's mother is the sister of King Balarama. She returns with her son and his wife, Vatsala, to her brother's palace, and seeks his forgiveness and understanding. As she is his sister, Balarama will honour her wishes. He was led astray by those Kauravas, whose life is spent in trying to prove they are mightier than the Pandavas . . . I am a Pandava too, and the honour of my family was at stake . . .'

And we were back at the ashram near Varanvata, where Ghatotkacha had deposited Princess Vatsala such a magically short while ago. Abhimanyu and Vatsala had stars in their eyes, and were looking like a couple in love from any time and age. Lady Subhadra appeared regal, and quite in charge of things.

'Dear Ghatotkacha, you are the pride of the Pandavas,' she murmured gratefully. My telepathic receptors seemed to be working overtime—I could perfectly understand what she was saying. 'And now it is time for us to go back to Dwarka and meet my brother Balarama to seek his blessing for his new son-in-law. I am certain he has repented and understood the futility of trying to get Vatsala married to that dolt Lakshmana!' She smiled mischievously, and for a moment looked like a young girl. Her eyes had a faraway gleam.

'Should I tell you a secret?' she went on. 'Many, many years ago, my brother Balarama had promised my hand in marriage to Lakshmana's father, Duryodhana! When Abhimanyu's father, Arjuna, came to visit my brother Krishna in Dwarka, though, we fell in love. But my brother Balarama had given his word to Duryodhana, who had been his favourite pupil. It was his word against my heart, and my heart won. Balarama is a kind and gentle man, and he relented once he understood that Arjuna had not run away with me—but that we had run away together! We lived together in Dwarka for a year, and then another year in the beautiful city of Pushkara . . .'

I noticed that she was blushing. Sweet! And what irony to have history repeating itself. Although Duryodhana couldn't be amused by this turn of events!

'It's all thanks to you, Ghatotkacha,' Subhadra continued. 'And from this day forward, you are like a son to me and a true brother to my beloved Abhimanyu!'

'We are family, Mother Subhadra,' Ghatotkacha replied, bending his tall frame in a graceful bow.

Another Pushpaka Vimana had materialized, and the tireless Ghatotkacha led Abhimanyu, Vatsala and Subhadra into it. As it soared to the sky, I was magically transported back to the cubbyhole where I had slept the night I found myself in this strange and inexplicable time and place.

Suddenly, I was desperately homesick and missing my familiar bedroom in Epic Apartments, with the photo of Bhaichung Bhutia on my bedside table, the faded Maradona poster on the wall and the sounds of traffic rising from all those floors below . . . I had no idea how much time had passed in this hectic romantic adventure. I was exhausted and longed to sleep, but before I dozed off I thought of the scene we had left behind us when we fled Dwarka—with all the fine clothes following us in a cloud of silk, and the Kauravas and their men left naked. I giggled uncontrollably and, despite my fatigue, wished I had been there to witness their distress and watch the comedy play out. Though mystified about everything else, there was one thing I knew for sure: I was rooting for the Pandavas all the way.

Rakshasa Stew

I dreamt of my mother, a Russian-to-Hindi translator, though sometimes a Hindi-to-Russian translator. She also reads Spanish and French, and translates from them as well. These are hard times for translators, she says, but she loves her work. She really does.

In my dream, Mum was looking into her mainframe computer and weeping. Then she looked through her piled-up dictionaries and wept some more. 'I can't find it,' she sobbed. 'I can't find the words!' And then I could see her face on the screen, wild-eyed and screwed-up with grief. 'I can't find him!' she wailed. 'He's lost! My son, Chintu, is lost!'

The dream continued as dreams do, wandering into inconsequential details, including the water monster I had encountered when I first arrived wherever it was that I had arrived. My father, Abhimanyu Dev Gupta, didn't figure in my dream; though I am sure he was weeping too, in his men-don't-weep way, wondering where I had disappeared.

I woke up feeling worried, and a bit guilty. Here I was, having the time of my life and the most incredible adventure, and my parents were going crazy wondering where I was. I remembered how worried my mother gets when the school bus returns me home late, or if I stay over too long at a friend's. My unexplained disappearance must be killing her, I concluded. I *had* to get out of here, get back to Gurgaon, somehow.

So, armed with my resolve to escape this fascinating time and place soon, I climbed down the rope ladder to catch up with Ghatotkacha and Hidimbi Ma. My breakfast arrived shortly: scrambled eggs and toast. Something more interesting was cooking in an enormous pot balanced over a boiling, crackling fire. It smelled delicious but it was much too high for me to peer into.

'What's cooking?' I asked cheerily. 'What's in the hot pot?'

Hidimbi Ma didn't normally reply to me directly. Ghatto and I had established our own mode of communication, but mind-reading and telepathic prompting was much more awkward with her.

'It's a traditional rakshasa stew,' she responded to me this time. 'Three types of animals and some fowl, but no humans. Absolutely NO humans. We gave that up after I married Lord Bhimasena . . . not even on feast days!'

Something in my circuitry just simply crashed. This. Was. Not. Real. She was—had been—a cannibal! I trusted Ghatotkacha and Hidimbi Ma, but what was to stop one of their rakshasa brethren from getting tempted by a tasty morsel of young human flesh?

'. . . wild boar, venison and baby squirrel,' she'd been continuing happily. 'You must try some!'

Clearly this was not *my* time and place.

A new thought struck me that afternoon. Perhaps it was like being trapped inside a simulation, a video game. Like in an interactive video game, if I played it right, I could get out the system!

Hidimbi Ma had observed my consternation. She picked me up and held me to her bosom. Today she smelled of my mother, of her favourite perfume, Chanel No. 5. Unbelievable. I began sobbing.

'I want t-t-to go home . . .' I whimpered. 'I want my mamma!'

'I'm like your mother too, little one,' she said consolingly.

Just a few sizes bigger, I thought to myself.

I clambered down from her chest, avoiding the jangly skull jewellery and her long braids, and tried very hard to compose myself. I was their guest and they had been more than kind to me. In an odd way, they had become family. *Yes, I am safe with them, and they will see me home*, I told myself.

'We will send you home, Chintu Pintu,' Ghatto said reassuringly. Then his tone turned thoughtful. 'It's just a matter of timing. There is one moment in the year, and only one, when it is possible to breach the veil of time. And the other thing is, we have to land you right—synchronous with when you left. There's also the matter of the movement of time in the Dwapara yuga running at a slightly different pace from Kali yuga time, as the earth now spins a little faster than it will in the future. I'm no good at maths and calculations, young un, but

I will ask the lady Dhumavati and her crows . . . We will journey there together!'

It was all very confusing, to be honest, but I knew Ghatto always meant what he said, and did it too. Looking up, I saw an enormous tear coursing down Hidimbi Ma's cheek.

'Your mother must be missing you, little boykin!' she said as softly as she could. 'We will send you back to your time. Whatever happens, however we can, we rakshasas will honour your human wish.' She wiped the tear from her face.

'Speaking of time . . .' she continued enthusiastically. 'Speaking of time, what moment better than the present? Let's go, Ghatotkacha, this very moment, to Ma Dhumavati, to seek her advice!'

Backward/Forward

We didn't fly through the air this time, but trudged through the forests and hills. The shadows eventually lengthened and the sun hung low on the horizon. After what seemed like a very long time, we reached a clearing atop a steep slope. A petite woman was sitting there, before the embers of a dying fire. She had grey hair, which had been left open and fell in cascades to her waist.

There was something strange about her. At first I couldn't put my finger on it. Then I realized what it was. She looked both very young and very old. She was wizened and wise, yet there was something vivacious in the way she leaned forward to welcome us.

'What brings you to this lonely spot?' she asked cordially. I could understand her loud and clear. 'The royal rakshasi Hidimbi and her noble son, Ghatotkacha—accompanied by a human child? Oh, my memory is failing me . . . a child from the Kali yuga . . .'

Hidimbi Ma fell prostrate at her feet. 'Dhumavati, the all-knowing, all-seeing Mahavidya Dhumavati, only you can help us,' she whispered. 'He has wandered here by mistake. Send him back to where he belongs!'

'Backward, forward . . . what does it matter?' Dhumavati said enigmatically. 'But I cannot see—there is still too much light around!' Vigorously, she shook her long hair about, forward and backward, this way and that. It fanned the embers of the dying fire, and dense smoke began rising around us, encircling us. We sat in silence in the engulfing darkness, waiting for Dhumavati to speak.

But she remained silent. I could hear her long, deep breathing and Hidimbi Ma's quick breaths. As the smoke cleared, I discovered that we were surrounded by a cloud of black crows. They examined us with beady, curious eyes, and then, suddenly, they began cawing. It was a sombre sound, the *caw-caw-caw-caw-caw* crowing merging and rising in a harsh, threatening crow chorus. They stopped as abruptly as they had begun, and flew away in all directions in a whoosh of flapping black feathers.

Dhumavati smiled at us. 'It shall be done,' she declared calmly. 'On the *amavasya* night of the coming month, the dark, moonless silence shall guide him back to the Kali yuga. Bring him here to me the evening before, and I shall make preparations . . .' She waved us away.

Two of the crows had remained behind, not having flown away with the rest. They sat perched on her shoulders, their watchful eyes alive with intelligence. I'd always thought crows were smart, but these were on a different level altogether. Sort of an Einstein at a TED Talk, if you get what I mean.

We walked back home—that was how I had begun to think if it. I wondered why we weren't flying any more. Ghatotkacha picked up on my thought and explained it with his usual thoughtfulness.

'We rakshasas have powers we ourselves don't understand,' he said. 'But we know that they get used up when we resort to magic and illusion, and also when we use kinetic energy'—*that* was the phrase he used—*kinetic energy!*—'to fly Pushpaka Vimanas or indeed to leap through the air like hawks and eagles. Most rakshasas get their strength from bloodthirst, and eating humans is very, very effective in recharging our powers. But since we—my mother and I—gave up human flesh, we have to seek spiritual strength, from other sources. So that's why we are taking a hike through the woods, buddy!'

What sort of energy sources? I wondered.

Ghatotkacha was quick with his reply. 'Earth strength,' he said, a note of deep conviction in his voice. 'Earth strength and sun strength, the powers of the wind, the blessings of the stars. My mother, Hidimbi Devi, is a rakshasi, but by marrying the mighty Pandava Bhima, she acquired human *samskaras* and the bonds of the human race. And I,' he pulled himself up to his full height as he said this, 'I am the son of Bhima, the grandson of Pandu and of Vayu, lord of the wind. My father's mother is the royal Kunti, daughter of Surasena, adopted by his

cousin Kuntibhoja. My brothers—whom I have never met—are
Sutasoma and Sarvaga. Need I say more? That is my strength, just
as my rakshasa heritage is my strength. But strength has to be
used with care and intelligence, or it shrivels up and turns upon
itself.'

My giant friend was getting philosophical, and I was getting
hungry.

Later, over a pot of delicious rakshasa stew under the firefly
chandelier, we talked about my return.

'We have eleven days before us,' he said, a tinge of sadness in
his voice. 'Let us use the time well. I shall show you the joys of
the forest, and we will have . . .' he struggled with the word '. . .
a-a *picnic* together!'

I thought of all the school picnics I had been to, in smelly
buses full of noisy kids (like myself). I smiled and gave him a
high five—not an easy feat given his height, but I jumped up to
reach his outstretched hand!

'A picnic it will be,' I declared. 'An eleven-day picnic!' Then
I remembered I had to be with Ma Dhumavati the night before
my 'departure'.

Ten days were all I had here, with Ghatotkacha.

So here it is, a diary of my days and nights in the forest.

The Secrets of the Forest

First, the sounds.

There is something about silence that makes every sound seem louder. And the forest is a very noisy and very silent place. It's not just birds chirping and lions roaring and elephants trumpeting. Sometimes when they all go quiet, one can hear the other sounds—the sounds of silence . . .

The first night we spent together in the forest, I was afraid, even though I had Ghatotkacha by my side. The stars were twinkling and sparking and blinking with a peculiar intensity, as though they were staring at us with a deep curiosity from millions of light years away. How many years later would they be shining down on our fifth-floor Gurgaon flat? Not that one can sight the stars from Gurgaon, anyway.

In a burst of enthusiasm, Ghatotkacha scrambled up a tall deodar tree. The needles scraped against my skin and I could smell the deep pine and resin fragrance, but I couldn't see much until we reached the very top branch and the starlight illuminated everything. We were as high up as my bedroom balcony, perhaps, but that's where the resemblance to anything in my twenty-first century existence ended.

The Milky Way was like a river of light above us. 'It's called the Aakash Ganga, the sky-river of the universe,' Ghatotkacha explained. Even as he spoke, streaks of light flashed across the heavens, like fireballs in a celestial Diwali display. This was, of course, a meteor shower; but never before had I felt so much a part of our universe on mother ship earth, as I did atop that deodar tree with my friend Ghatotkacha.

I could hear a strange rustling, like that of dry leaves rubbing against each other in the undergrowth. Then I realized that it was emanating from Ghatotkacha. Next, in flashes of light from the meteor shower, I could see a gauzy gossamer net stretching from our treetop to the next. On closer examination, I discovered a dozen busy spiders deftly constructing a vast web.

There it was, a silken hammock spread across the forest canopy. Unbelievably, it could take our combined weight—of Ghatotkacha's giant body and my considerably smaller one. We lay cradled in the spiderweb and swung dreamily between the deodar trees.

'Sleep well, my sons!' one of the trees said to us in a kind and gentle voice.

'Be safe between the heavens and Mother Earth,' another whispered. It had a scratchy sort of voice, as though it had a sore throat.

'These trees can talk?' I asked, wonderstruck.

'Deodars are the most noble of trees,' Ghatotkacha replied. 'They can listen, speak, pray and dance. It is a blessing to sleep in their midst, and the blessing shall stay with you all your life, Chintu Pintu!'

And spiders? I wondered. *Can spiders speak too?*

'Haven't you heard of the silence of the spiders?' Ghatotkacha replied, genuinely surprised by my ignorance. 'Spiders are denied the power of speech, all except the hungry cannibal spiders, who can hiss and shriek to terrify and immobilize their victims before they attack!'

I was *sort of* getting the heebie-jeebies. 'Are we safe here?' I asked anxiously. 'I mean, *you* are safe, naturally, and I'm safe because I'm with you . . . but is it okay to be in a spiderweb high up in the sky? Won't they try to trap us?'

'I saved the spiders from a huge spot of trouble some years ago,' Ghatotkacha answered sleepily. 'I'll tell you the story another time. But they are my friends and allies now. And they are masters of illusions too, in their own way. They can't hear, for they don't have ears like mine . . . but they can pick up on vibrations! Listen!'

He made the same sound he had earlier, like leaves rustling, and the dozen spiders that had been waiting patiently at the edges of the web scurried around in a sudden burst of energy.

'Ugh!' I screamed. 'I don't like spiders!'

'Like them or not, you can learn from them, as you can from everyone and everything in the forest,' Ghatotkacha added, in what I had come to regard as his schoolmaster voice. 'The silence of the spiders is the secret of their powers. Which creature would innocently venture into their cunning nests if they sat waiting with noise or speech? Sometimes you—or at least I—can hear them tapping their toes on the rocks, or clapping their two palps to announce themselves. But when they weave their invisible nets, they are as silent as the night, for their silence is the secret to their subterfuge.'

Indeed the night was silent, at least until Ghatotkacha's high-pitched snores broke the tranquil quietude. That night, I dreamt of my mother again—that she was missing me, and weeping.

I woke up to what had to be the most enthusiastic birds in the world. They twittered and tweeted and warbled and trilled and chirred and cheeped and squeaked and piped and peeped and chirruped and whistled! It was quite exhausting, though, especially as I was all knotted up inside and wondering momentarily what I was doing in a spider nest atop a deodar tree with a giant rakshasa, even though I had grown to like and respect him enormously. I peered down at the ground below. It seemed an inconceivable distance away.

'I want to get down, back to earth,' I muttered. 'I'm NOT an insect and I DON'T like spiderwebs. And insects shouldn't either if they have any sense!'

Ghatotkacha sensed my mood and tried to distract me. 'Have you ever bent a sunbeam, young un?' he asked. 'Let me show you how it's done . . . it's the happiest wake-up workout in the world!'

It worked.

The rays of the morning sun were dancing around us, golden arrows of light with radiant motes of glowing dust circling them. They were like specks of gold with a pale rainbow border. I watched, fascinated, as Ghatotkacha shut his eyes and made a low humming sound from deep in his throat. The little globes of gold dust began to hop and skip around, and the sunbeams too changed their pattern and direction. Suddenly there was a golden ladder below us, from the spiderweb right to the ground. The rays of sunlight, the motes of dust—all appeared normal again, as before, but a bit of their light had been diverted to the sunbeam ladder below.

'A mote of dust, dangling on a sunbeam . . . that's what our earth is, young un,' he continued. 'Do you understand?'

To be frank, I didn't. I was beyond astonishment by now.

We climbed down, my rakshasa companion and I, step by step. I didn't ask him how he had done it, and he didn't bother to explain. It was only when we had reached level ground that he threw light on his incredible feat.

'It's to do with the laws of physics,' he said, in our by-now easy two-way translation mode. 'Matter is malleable, and the morning sunshine is the most supporting and nurturing energy in the world.'

Now, what was I to say to that? 'I'm hungry, Ghatto!' is how I responded. 'What's for breakfast?'

The next day was spent in the company of gandharvas and kinnaras. These beautiful angelic tribes rarely mingled with the rough rakshasa lot, but then Ghatotkacha was no ordinary rakshasa—he was also a Pandava, and son of the strongest warrior in the world.

'The joys of the gandharvas cannot be shared by mortals, much less rakshasas,' Ghatotkacha had cautioned me. 'Our time together will pass as a dream, and be obliterated from memory when we leave.'

That was indeed what happened. A rainbow was spread across the sky, and I remember seeing colours that I had never imagined existed. Haunting music lingers in my ears, and a taste of sweetness in my mouth. And that is all.

We set out on foot that night, my rakshasa friend and I. He walked in slow, measured steps to keep pace with me, but refrained from picking me up and carrying me on his shoulders or like a bundle in his arms. It was the darkest night I have never known. Perhaps the clouds had shut out the sky and the moon and the starlight. We walked along the curve of a hill. I could sense, rather than see, the ravine below.

'Don't be afraid, Chintu Pintu,' Ghatotkacha reassured me. 'Remember, we forest dwellers don't need light to see? Our ears, our nose, our skin—we can see with them just as well.'

Ghatto tapped his enormous jug-shaped ears and a gold-and-brass helmet materialized around his head. It had a small green jewel mounted on it. He tapped the gem and a weak light illuminated the path before us. But still, the occasional shriek of a night creature, a scurrying animal, the gleam of faraway feral eyes—these things gave me no reassurance or comfort. I was not afraid—how could I be, with mighty Ghatotkacha beside me?—but rather, I was apprehensive. Boys from Gurgaon didn't belong here, not this one at least. Here, I had the sense of a lonely spinning planet, alone in its orbit, sheltering all kinds of creatures. This was not the earth of my age, which belonged to us humans alone. Here there were no satellites, no Internet, no cordoned-off national parks, no national highways. Man had not tamed the planet yet, then.

The path went on and on, close to the hill, hugging it along the turns of the forested slope. The emerald light faltered and blinked as it continued to guide my—our—way.

Suddenly, there was noise, and bustle, and light.

I wasn't sure about the source of the dazzling light. It wasn't like sunlight, more perhaps like the white light from a CFL bulb. I realized, to my surprise, that this light cast no shadows. There were blazing torches set in a circle around the lit-up area, and then, around that, all was dark.

Ghatotkacha and I took the scene in. An extremely thin man with matted hair sat cross-legged upon a throne-like low golden seat covered with deerskin. Young men draped in flowing white robes were seated in a circle around him, some of them facing his motionless back. His eyes were closed, and he seemed to be lost in deep meditation. His tangled locks were motionless too; they were set in a sort of bun on his head and the rest flowed all the way down to a deerskin rug. The bones in his chest were visible, the ribcage perfectly defined, the stomach held in. Yet there was no sign that he was breathing; there was no rise and fall of the chest as might have been expected. An enormous insect, somewhere between a beetle and a dragonfly, had settled on his hair, but he seemed not to have noticed.

The young men were chanting melodiously in what I could recognize as Sanskrit, though it has never been my favourite subject at school. There was a trance-like feel about it all. The island of light in the dark night; the sea of stars above us; the dense silence broken by the beauty of the chanting; the holy man with the matted hair, still silent, his eyes still shut. Was he even breathing?

Suddenly a third eye appeared on his calm brow and began examining me. Ghatotkacha and me, I suppose, as my friend was so much larger than me. But the eye looked angry, as if disturbed by our intrusion.

I nudged Ghatotkacha. 'Let's leave,' I whispered. 'I don't have a good feeling about this!'

So we returned to the winding path along the edge of the hill.

'He looked mad . . .' I said. 'Who was he? And who were they?'

'He is Rishi Vrischika, the most revered and feared of sages. This is the time of the year when Scorpius, the constellation of Vrischika, is in the ascendant. He went into samadhi twenty-two years ago, but his students and disciples gather around him to gain knowledge and strength.'

'Samadhi?' I asked. 'Does that mean he is dead? How can a dead man open his eyes and give us such a dirty look?' I had never actually seen a dead man before. That's not how dead people looked in newspaper photographs or on television. I was agitated, even frightened now.

'Hush, young man! Humans live, humans die; but the great and evolved rishis and the race of immortals are different. They can control life and what you call "death". Even we rakshasas are different. We don't surrender all our life force when we "die"—some things remain in the body and around it. Don't worry about it—things are different in the Kali yuga, from where you come.'

'He was dead but he could SEE us? How can anybody be dead but *not* dead?'

We were walking steadily in the dark. Where was Ghatotkacha taking me? I was tired, confused. And afraid.

'It's sort of like . . . a battery from your times,' he explained. 'A battery is dead, but it can be recharged—can't it?'

'And what do *you* know about batteries, Mr Gentle Giant?' I asked in exasperation. 'I haven't seen one around here since I landed up!' It was all simply too puzzling.

Just then, the dawn broke and a calm blue light appeared at the horizon.

'You are tired, Chintu Pintu,' Ghatotkacha said gently. 'This was a path we had to walk at night. Now that the goddess of dawn, Ushas, has lit up the sky, it is time for us to sleep.'

I wondered why it was that we had to walk this trail at night, but I was too bushed to ask. Walking to the clearing ahead, we lay down in the soft, damp grass and fell asleep, boy and rakshasa, as the birds twittered and sang to welcome the day.

I didn't dream of my mother or of Gurgaon—instead, my dreams were full of the time we had spent in Dwarka with the beautiful princess Vatsala. I dreamt of Duryodhana and his son Lakshmana, and the look on the older Kaurava's face as we had flown away from the crowded assembly hall where the marriage was to have been celebrated. I awoke with a sense of foreboding. The look in Duryodhana's eyes would not leave me; it stayed in my imagination along with the look in the sage Vrischika's eyes—his long-dead eyes, glowering at me . . .

My anxious musings were interrupted as Ghatto took me by the hand and we began our march again.

'Where are we going now?' I asked, or rather moaned, as we started trudging once more through the forest, my mind racing. *What's happened to Ghatotkacha's magic—to his power of illusions, to Pushpaka Vimanas whizzing across the skies, to the pizzas and the comfort food that materialized so effortlessly?*

'This is a pilgrimage, my dear Chintu. We are going on a pilgrimage so that when you return to your times, you will take back the gift of knowledge from the past. And knowledge does not come without effort, perseverance and suffering. So be patient, and follow me.'

'You sound like our assistant headmaster, Mr Ruchir Ramesh,' I responded sullenly. This was turning out to be the opposite of the picnic I thought we had set out on!

Ghatotkacha ignored my comment. 'My ancestor Trikaalini imparted to me the gift of prescience—I can sense, even if I do not know, the future. You *will* return, Chintu Pintu, to your mother and father in the blink of an eye, and your family will forget that you had wandered so far in time from them.'

Now, that reassured me. I had been worrying about the journey back—it sounded like an improbable, if not impossible, task to relocate me precisely where I had left off. I did not want to be a lost-in-time traveller, overshooting the mark and arriving in some improbable sci-fi future, or even missing it just a bit and landing up in Akbar's court or in the middle of the Kalinga War or during the Crusades! What if I was to return to the future and land in America before Columbus, in the heart of an Apache tribe? That might even be fun . . .

Quit fooling around, I told myself sternly. *This is serious!* Serious *serious.* In truth, I longed, in every cell of my being, to be back where I once belonged.

For we belong, each of us, in a time and place. Our ideas, our way of understanding things come from that conditioning. This much I'd figured out. Just from all that I knew of the past from the Amar Chitra Katha comics I had read, the television serials I had watched, the grandmother's tales that had been recited to me, could I make sense of these mysterious times I had arrived in? Even with some help from my rakshasa friend?

Because even though I wanted to be home, somewhere, somehow, knowing Ghatotkacha, his strength and his nobility, had made me loyal to him and the age he lived in. Even towards the end of that day I could not forget the image of the dead sage Vrischika glaring at me with his third eye. What's more, I imagined myself cross-legged in space, hurtling among the stars and the debris of comets. Despite Ghatto's uncertain foresight, surely anything *could* happen on the journey back? And then I began to wonder if it was necessary to go back at all.

Can't I just continue living here? In these times, with Ghatotkacha and Hidimbi Ma as my adopted family?

Every evening, as the waning moon appeared on the horizon, I would be struck by uncertainty and anxiety, overtaken by panic. And then Ghatotkacha would cheer me up, as only he could, by whistling a cheerful tune or rustling up—finally!—a magical plate of pepperoni pizza.

So what do I remember most about those days and nights in the forest?

I remember the night skies and, in the sky, the waning moon. I felt the moon talked to me here; it was not the grimy yellow

thing in the sky I glimpsed from my balcony. And I remember the nakshatra Rohini.

'It is called Aldebaran in your times,' Ghatotkacha once explained. 'Rohini is a fixed star. On either side are the stars Soma and Agni. They are sisters, and they stand for food, appetite and health. And beside them are Rudra and Yama, the gods of destruction and death.'

I remember that I didn't want to think of Yama, the lord of death. I just didn't.

'I'm afraid,' I said to Ghatotkacha. I was whispering, almost weeping. 'I'm scared to death that I will die on the journey back home. Suppose I explode or implode or get stuck in space or in the molten lava bubbling inside the earth?'

Ghatotkacha lifted me up in his arms so I could see his rough, kind face, the enormous ears, the jewel on his forehead.

'NOTHING EVER DIES,' he said gently, and I could sense that he was speaking to me in capital letters. 'Remember, nothing ever dies. Look at the moon—you would think it has died, it has disappeared . . . but it waxes and wanes and waxes again. You might think it has died, but it returns.'

Lord Bhimasena

Dawn was breaking in the eastern sky. I had lost count of our days in the forest; and though I wasn't convinced about returning to the Kali yuga yet, I was less afraid than I had been. The morning breeze was ruffling the branches of the tall trees

around us. It was almost as if they were waving their arms and wishing us good morning. That's when Ghatotkacha's enormous ears began flapping in the strangest way—in all directions, like they were trying to catch the wind. He had an intent expression on his face, like he was listening to an unseen voice. He seemed concerned yet excited, and before I could ask him what the matter was, he had scooped me up in his arms, and there we were—flying over the hilltops, with the sky above us and the wind in our ears.

'Er, where are we going?' I asked timidly. Ghatotkacha looked preoccupied, more so than I had ever known him to be.

'It's my father,' he replied. 'My father, Lord Bhimasena. He is lost in the forest and in trouble. We must find him, rescue him!'

I liked the way he said 'we'. I wasn't doing much after all, except being carried about.

We arrived in no time at all, hovering above a nearby forest top. The weather had changed dramatically in our short flight. A hailstorm was lashing the tall deodars, which were shivering and shaking as though in a kind of demented trance. We landed in a mess of sleet and hailstones—more and more were showering

down on us, each the size of a golf ball. I spotted a group of men sheltering under the rough cover of some extended branches. They wore a sort of barkcloth kilt wrapped around their loins, and carried the most massive bows and arrows, not made of bent bamboo as one might have imagined, but crafted with gold and silver and embossed with precious stones. There was something in their bearing as well—their strong, perfectly toned bodies and their proud, straight-backed demeanour—that alerted me to the fact that these were no ordinary mortals. Sitting on a boulder beside them was a strikingly lovely woman, with long black hair framing her beautiful, imperious face. Her hair was streaming wet and, although she was huddled under the rain and the hail, I could see that it reached all the way to her knees.

The tallest among them resembled the lordly figure of Duryodhana, whom I had last seen in Dwarka's court. Of the others, one was squat, muscular and built like a bull. I could see the awesome strength that rippled through his muscles even when he was still and sheltering from nature's onslaught. His eyes were gentle—not the fierce ones of a warrior, which he proved to be with that staggeringly strong build. His eyes reminded me of someone . . . but who? And then I knew. These were Ghatotkacha's eyes—the tender, humane eyes of my kind and compassionate rakshasa friend.

It came to me in a flash: this was none other than Bhima— Lord Bhimasena! The tall man was Yudhishthira, and the two handsome young men standing with them were surely Nakula and Sahadeva. *But where's Arjuna then?* I wondered.

Ghatotkacha did not waste any time with words, and neither did he give any indication that he had recognized the Pandavas. Instead he bent low in supplication. And then with the elan and skill of a practised magician, he produced, out of nowhere, a bark canopy covered with what at first appeared to be raindrops but on closer inspection were like the shining crystals that had decorated the buildings in Dwarka.

'This should make your journey easier,' he said in a tone of utmost politeness.

Even as the men moved out from under the sheltering branches, a fine palanquin, covered in purple silk, materialized—its four ends were joined together in a single pole at the bottom. Ghatotkacha entreated the lady to step inside and sit back on the soft pillowed seat, and held it aloft in his arms.

Then he gestured to me that I should get under the bark canopy as well. So there I was, Chintu Pintu from Gurgaon, reaching just above the Pandavas' waists, trudging along a damp and muddy path with the greatest warriors on earth.

The hailstorm ceased after some time, but it was still raining heavily. We walked downhill, then uphill, until we reached a small cave with a clearing in front. Ghatotkacha balanced the lady's palanquin against a rock and ventured into the cave's mouth—he had to squeeze a bit to get in. We could hear him clapping loudly inside the cave, and I wondered what he was doing. Then he emerged and patiently stood by the opening. A bear rushed out, and then two more! I was terrified, but it was reassuring to be with these tall, strong men, with their taut bows and fatal arrows, ready for any trouble.

Then my rakshasa friend led us into the dark cave, which had a strange musty odour with hints of herb as well as smoke. Ghatotkacha lit a fire and as the flames leapt up, I could see some beautiful paintings on the roof of the cave—of birds and beasts, and gorgeous apsaras with their hands folded in prayer. The cave had clearly been inhabited before, perhaps by some rishis and holy men. A silver platter with a variety of fruits materialized magically by the fire. The stale smell disappeared in an instant, and it was warm and cheery inside the rocky walls of the cave.

The tall man, the one who reminded me of Duryodhana, bent low and folded his hands to thank us. He had a deep, kind voice. I could understand his words clearly, as though I was reading

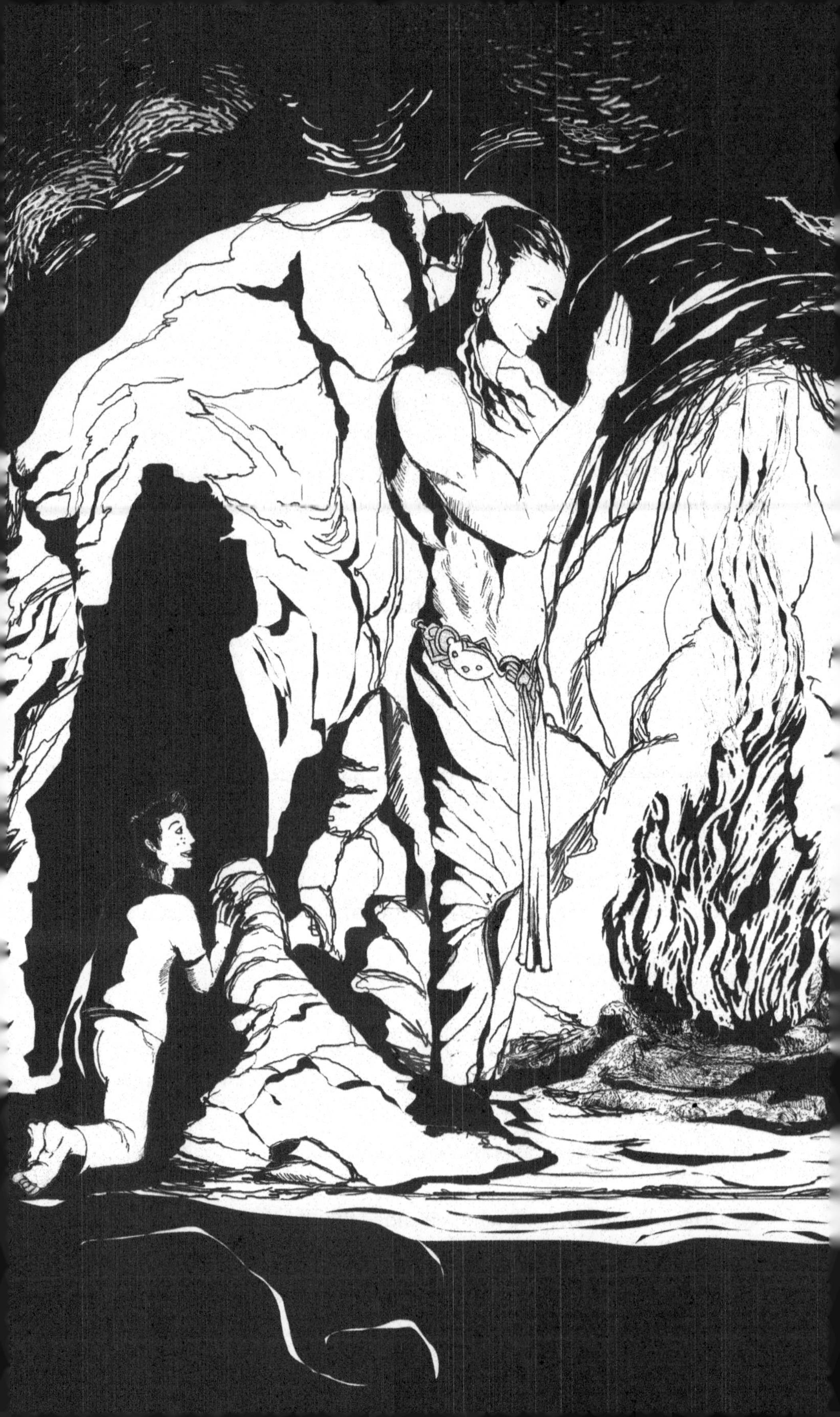

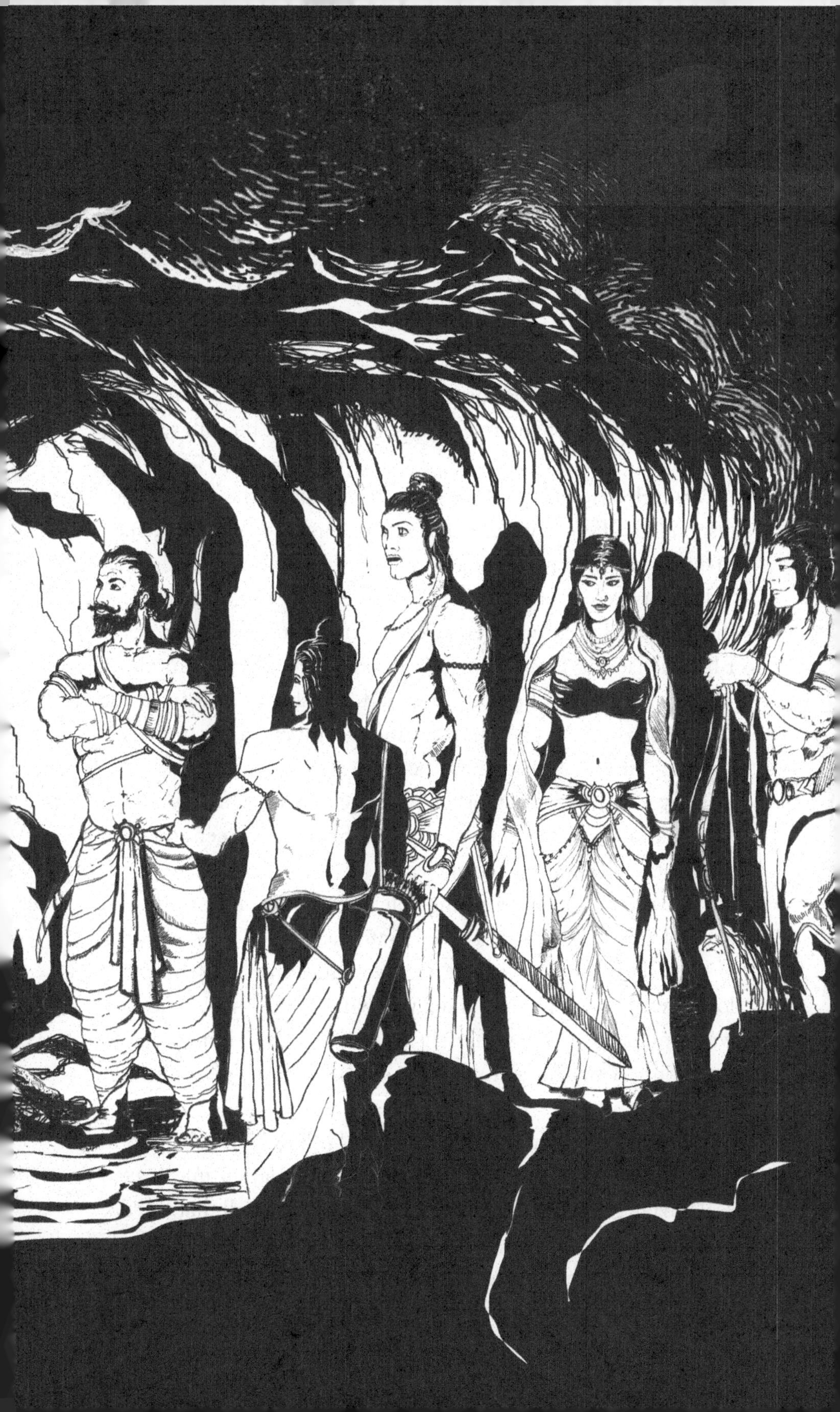

the subtitles during a film. 'I am Yudhishthira,' he said, 'of the Pandava clan. These are my brothers, the lords Bhimasena, Nakula and Sahadeva. Our brother the noble Arjuna is not with us—he is in Indraloka with his father, Indra, lord of the heavens. We thank you for your help and shall always carry a debt of gratitude to you.'

Ghatotkacha drew himself up to his full height. 'I am Ghatotkacha,' he announced, 'son of Hidimbi Ma and Lord Bhimasena of the Pandavas. Thank you for your blessings, which I cherish.'

An electric atmosphere spread through the cave. They responded differently, each of them. Yudhishthira's eyes widened in surprise, but his expression remained calm. Nakula and Sahadeva were both clearly delighted and also intrigued by this unexpected announcement. As for Ghatotkacha's father—Bhimasena—his face furrowed in a complicated mix of emotions. There was astonishment and joy and also a sort of pain in his face. His eyes filled up with tears and he embraced Ghatotkacha, hugging him for a very long time.

'My son,' he said with a sort of disbelief. 'My son! My son!'

Ghatotkacha bent down to touch his father's feet and then sought the blessings of his uncles.

'How handsome my young son looks! And how strong and gentle he is! I am proud of you, Ghatotkacha!'

The lady with the striking eyes and the long hair left loose, who was clearly Draupadi, wife of the five Pandavas, was watching expressionlessly as this human drama played itself out. Now she summoned Ghatotkacha to give him her blessings.

'Give my greetings to your mother, Hidimbi Ma,' she said in a melodious voice that was somehow pitched at an unexpected scale. 'May glory and good luck accompany you in all that you do.'

'We must leave now,' Ghatto said. 'My revered father has only to think of me and I shall be there before him to do as he pleases.

At war or in peace, my life is at his command.' My friend bent down to touch her feet. His expression was impassive yet his eyes were troubled.

And so we left the royal wanderers in the cave and stepped out. It was still pouring. Ghatotkacha picked me up in his arms and we flew through the air, sheathed in something like a gossamer spiderweb. To my surprise, we did not return to the lonely path high in the mountains where we had been travelling earlier. Instead we were close to the forest clearing where Hidimbi Ma lived, in the house timbered with tall sal trees.

Upon landing, we sat down on a mighty tree trunk that lay on the ground like a gigantic natural bench. The rain had stopped. It was calm and quiet, and birds were chirruping around us. Next to me, Ghatotkacha was silent and moody. He seemed to be brooding about something.

'He did not mention my mother,' he said at last. 'My father did not ask after my mother—not even once!'

I didn't know how to respond. How would I have felt if that had happened to me?

I thought of my parents, and how they had seemed to be happy together once, before things had begun to go wrong. Then I remembered their fights and their silences, and I felt very sorry for Ghatotkacha, and for myself. I clambered up his shoulders and put my arms around his sinewy neck. There was not much I could say.

We returned home as the sun was slipping into the shadows of the mountains. Hidimbi Ma was busy digging up roots and tubers in a corner of her garden. Her face lit up with a most bewitching smile when she saw us approaching.

'I have met my royal father,' Ghatotkacha reported impassively. 'And my uncles, the Pandavas. I am glad I could be of service to them.'

Her eyes widened with elation. 'How is he?' she questioned eagerly. 'Did he ask about me?'

'Lord Bhimasena inquired about you,' Ghatotkacha replied without hesitation, forcing a smile to his lips. 'He sent you his greetings and said he will come and visit you soon.'

Tears welled up in her lustrous eyes and settled like giant dewdrops on her long lashes. 'Your father is the handsomest and strongest man in the world,' she murmured. 'I was blessed to have been his wife, even if not for long.'

She turned to me, the sweetest smile still playing on her lips. 'Let me tell you a story,' she said. 'A story about the mightiest man in the world, and about how I fell in love with him. My brother, Hidimb, wanted to kill Lord Bhimasena—as if that were possible!—and roast him for dinner. But it was not to be! We were destined to get married, me and Lord Bhima, and to have the strongest, gentlest, most courageous son in the world. It's a love story I am telling you, Chintu Pintu, because it's love that makes the world go round!'

There are so many images that have remained with me of those days; I remember it all so vividly. Even after all this time, I cannot forget that memorable evening when I found Ghatotkacha nonchalantly kicking around a ball. In a glade by the edge of the forest, I was sitting on a fallen log, watching the spectacular sunset, when Ghatto ambled into view before me with his toy. It was a humongous football, in keeping with his gigantic size. My own battered, well-punched playmate would have been but the size of a marble to him.

Well, he was dribbling it along and whistling to himself. When he saw me, he hurled the ball midfield, as though he had been playing football all his life. But, let it be said, if there was a net, I would have dived and saved the goal.

Anyway, I rose excitedly, only to find that the 'ball' was a swirling mass of coiled snakes, with their bright eyes and hissing fangs speckling the massive spherical surface! Naturally, terrified, I ran away as fast as I could from the scene.

My friend caught up with me later. 'Don't be afraid.' He was grinning. 'The serpents enjoy the game as much as I do!'

I was dumbfounded, to say the least. Snake football was NOT my chosen game, I explained. Nor would I ever be enthused by python cricket or cobra kabaddi, just to be clear.

'Every game has an element of danger,' he said, a serious note entering his voice. 'Remember, Chintamani, the real challenge is in keeping it a sport.'

He had called me Chintamani. I felt incredibly wise and grown-up just then, and later, in another time and place, I would remember and cherish his words.

The Time Crystal

The days fled by and I had given up keeping count of them. The waning moon was now a thin shadow of its former self. The thought that this enchanted adventure was about to come to an end made me truly sad. The idea of returning home—which seemed a faraway place—was shadowed by my terror of the journey back. I tried not to think about it but it was always there at the back of my mind, a constant sense of fear I did my best to forget and ignore.

It was then, in those last days there, that Ghatotkacha received a message from Bhima seeking his help. I do not quite know how it happened, but my friend 'heard' or 'saw' that his father was summoning him.

'We must set off,' he said to me, and there I was in his arms as we made our way across the wooded hills. We landed on the bank of a serene lake. All was still and silent around us. *Why has Bhima called us here?* There was no sign of him anywhere.

We studied our surroundings, taking in the beauty of the place. The lake was afloat with the most glorious and fragrant flowers I had ever seen. They looked like lotus flowers, but were much, much larger—each as large as a football, really. They smelled heavenly, as though all the scents of all the flowers in the world had been mixed and jumbled up—the sort of concoction you could encounter at the fragrance counter in an airport in our times.

A swarm of bees were buzzing about, drunk with the lovely smells. Everything else seemed quite normal, and Lord Bhima was still nowhere in sight. We were walking along the lakeshore, inhaling those maddening aromas, when we encountered a group of very tall men—almost as tall as Ghatotkacha—standing together in a circle. When they saw Ghatotkacha, they bowed low before him.

'Lord of the rakshasas!' they declared in their gruff voices. It took me a moment to make sense of the unfamiliar sounds. 'Protector of the Nishadha race! O Ghatotkacha, grant us your blessings!'

As they were thus bent down, I discovered a strong, muscular man in a barkcloth kilt standing in the centre of the circle. It was Ghatotkacha's dad, Bhimasena, himself! And he was looking a bit surprised by the respect his son commanded among these gigantic men.

'Father!' Ghatotkacha exclaimed and leapt through the posse of men to clutch at Bhima's feet. 'Revered Lord Bhimasena! I am at your service. What can I do for you?'

'Tell these men, who are so devoted to you, to stop treating me like a thief!' Lord Bhima responded, a note of irritation in his voice. 'I have come here in search of the Brahma Kamal, the thousand-petalled lotus. My lady Draupadi commanded me to find her some of these flowers so she could lose herself in their exquisite fragrance. Women are like that, you know—when they want something, they want it. So I came here in search of the flowers, and now these gentlemen claim I am stealing them!'

'We are the guardians of this lake, in the service of Lord Kubera,' one of the giant men replied. 'It is our duty to see that no one lays hands on these sacred flowers!'

'This is my father!' Ghatotkacha replied angrily. 'Ask for his forgiveness or you will not get mine!'

They immediately cowered when they heard that, and started grovelling before the Pandava prince for his pardon.

Bhima embraced Ghatotkacha. 'I wanted to see you again, my son,' he said, his voice brimming over with emotion. 'My eldest, my worthiest son!'

Tears were coursing down Ghatotkacha's cheeks. And Bhima's too. They were both softies, I decided, feeling a bit teary myself.

'And now it is time for me to leave,' Bhima said, his voice now weighed down with sadness and regret.

'We shall meet again,' Ghatotkacha whispered. 'And remember, my revered father, that I shall give my life for you if I have to.'

It was then that a strange-looking man came into sight. He was short and fair-skinned, and had a prominent pot belly. He was covered in jewels—dangling gold necklaces with shining gems; heavy, shimmering armbands—and he carried a jewelled pot, overflowing with what looked like ropes of gold and diamonds, like a handbag.

I observed him closely. And it got curiouser and curiouser. He had just one eye, which was a nasty yellow colour, and three legs. In spite of all these oddities, he seemed cheerful and good-natured.

'Welcome, Lord Bhima, to the garden of Chitraratha,' he said in a formal, ceremonious sort of voice. 'The thousand-petalled lotus flowers bloom only to greet you!'

'Greetings, Lord Kubera, master of wealth and glory!' Bhima replied. 'I had come here in search of just such a Brahma Kamal for the royal Draupadi, wife of the Pandavas. But your chaps tried to hold me back and arrest me. Thankfully my son Ghatotkacha turned up, and here I am, with a handful of flowers for my lady Draupadi . . .'

Kubera's face twitched with all sorts of emotions. I noticed he had a pair of small tusks protruding from below his nostrils. He clapped his small hands once, twice, thrice. 'Get every flower in the lake and produce it here before Lord Bhimasena of the Pandavas,' he declared. 'Mine is the palace of plenty . . . more Brahma Kamals will bloom faster than we can pluck them!'

A plump mongoose by Kubera's side scurried off with the guards, and soon they returned with basketfuls of the fragrant flowers.

'I must be going,' Bhimasena said impatiently. 'Besides, I wanted just one flower. I will take a basketful with me, and the others,' he paused to glance absent-mindedly at Ghatotkacha and me, 'my son and the boy can take back with them.'

And with that he set off, with long, sure strides down the mountain path. The flowers in the lake were blooming again, and we had three reed baskets before us.

Kubera looked at us curiously. 'Quite a pair, aren't you?' He giggled. 'Big and small, tall and tiny. Brothers?'

'My brothers are the sons of the Pandavas,' Ghatotkacha replied courteously. 'This is my friend Chintu Pintu, from this earth but a time in the future—from the Kali yuga.'

Lord Kubera stared at me with deep interest. 'So, Chintu Pintu, you want to get back to your time, don't you? I am Digpala, one of the lords of the eight directions, and I shall guide you back. Back to the future! Here is a time crystal—it contains the secrets of the future and the present. Not the past, for that is another story altogether. Hold on to it tightly when that old lady Dhumavati pushes you into the time-serpent's entrails.'

The time-serpent's entrails! The very thought made me shudder with fear. And how did he know about Dhumavati?

'Don't be afraid, Chintu Pintu,' Kubera said kindly. 'It's like turning a somersault in the air and making sure you land on your feet—or at least on your hands!'

I haven't yet forgotten that moment. Ghatotkacha towering beside me, Kubera and his mongoose by my side. The sun setting in the west, leaving a trail of unbelievable colours in the sky. The baskets of Brahma Kamals suffusing the air with a heavenly redolence. The time crystal in my hand—a small, translucent pebble that seemed to throb with a frequency that was both fast and slow, a measured beat that was quick yet quietly melodious. It put me at ease somehow, and I just hoped to God that it worked.

So we took our leave of Kubera, king of wealth, lord of the eight directions. Ghatotkacha carried the baskets of blooming lotuses in a sort of improvised cape and I sat on his shoulder as we sped through the air, the time crystal clutched in my fist.

Hidimbi Ma was excited to see us return carrying armloads of the exquisite scented flowers. Her eyes lit up and I could see how beautiful she must have been once, in her own way.

'For me, for me!' she chanted. 'My son has got me flowers!' Clapping her hands in delight, she took in deep, long breaths to inhale the intoxicating smell of Kubera's thousand-petalled lotuses.

'They are from my father, Lord Bhima,' Ghatotkacha said gently. 'For you.'

There was disbelief in her eyes, then joy. A tear trickled down, then another. She said nothing, and we sat there, each of us lost in our separate thoughts.

I was thinking of home, of my parents and if I would get to see them again. Hidimbi was surely lost in memories of her husband, Bhimasena, and the time they had once spent together. What an odd couple they must have been! And Ghatotkacha? He was brooding, I felt, about his father—his ever-absent, adored father, and all the things he would have liked to share with him.

Bhima was not your average dad, I reflected. Would I have been able to cope in Ghatotkacha's situation? Probably . . . no, certainly not. But how it did it matter? For now it was almost time to go, to return, to re-enter the tempest of time and find my own life, the one I had left behind.

The day arrived. A calm golden dawn broke in the eastern sky, illuminating a hilltop here, a mountainside there. It was a perfect day, with the sky a shade of blue that I still dream about sometimes, just before I awake.

Hidimbi Ma cooked me a delicious meal, a stewpot of meats and vegetables that simmered and bubbled all morning. *This is your last day here, Chintu Pintu*, I told myself again and again as I ate, pinching my arm to make myself realize that this was indeed real and not a dream.

Later, we went and played ducks and drakes by the lake, the same lake from which I had surfaced to find myself in Ghatotkacha's arms. We skimmed the stones across the waves, and they danced and jumped until the depths of the lake claimed them. I chose flat, round stones, and I remember they had a faint purple tinge to them. Ghatotkacha's stones went further than mine; in fact, they skipped confidently right to the other shore.

It was here, by the lake, that Dhumavati was to prepare for my journey back. She arrived as the evening was settling in, followed by a cloud of crows. I remembered how my English teacher, Ms Khanna, had told us that a gathering of crows was called a 'murder of crows'. The memory of her words alarmed me.

I held the stone that Kubera had given me in my hand, which still beat and throbbed with a life of its own. It was as if it had a heart and a mind, perhaps a soul as well. Kubera had called it a time crystal, and it was heartening that the lord of the eight directions had assigned it to see me home.

Looking up, I saw that Dhumavati had lit a smoky fire, and a carved brass vessel, surrounded by stones, had been placed by the side of the burning embers. Ghatotkacha and Hidimbi Ma were standing by the shadows, their tall figures still as statues.

'Have this tea, my son,' Dhumavati said in a kindly voice, and gave me some of the warm brew.

I started feeling very sleepy suddenly, as though I had run a marathon and had a hot bath and a glass of milk and settled into a soft bed. I could hear the whir of wings and had a sense of being carried through the air, or underwater—I couldn't tell which. It was like a gentle vortex at first, but it began spinning faster and faster, like a tornado hurtling through time. Ma Dhumavati's voice was in my ear.

'Take care, child,' she whispered. 'Worry not. All will be well.'

And another voice, one I had grown to know so well.

'Farewell, young un. We shall meet again.'

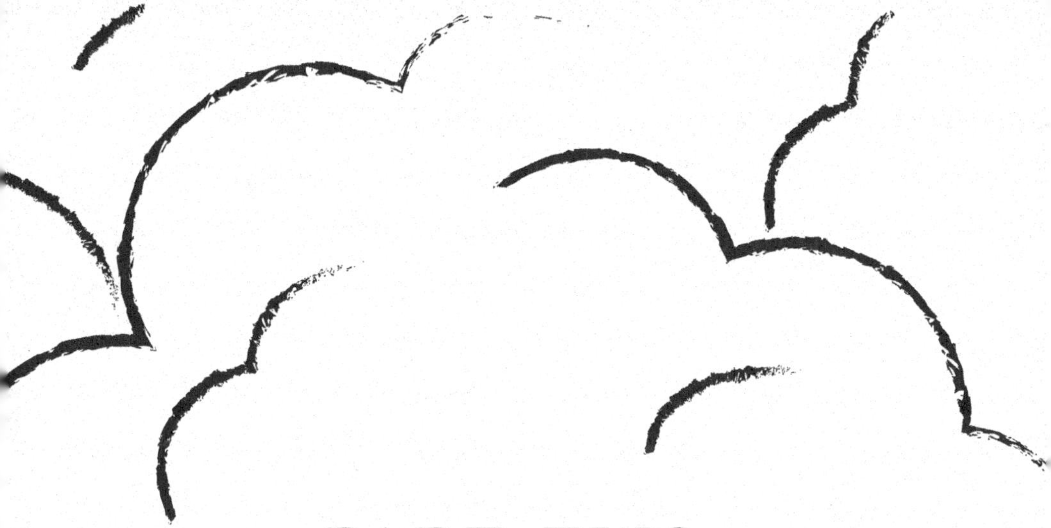

PART TWO

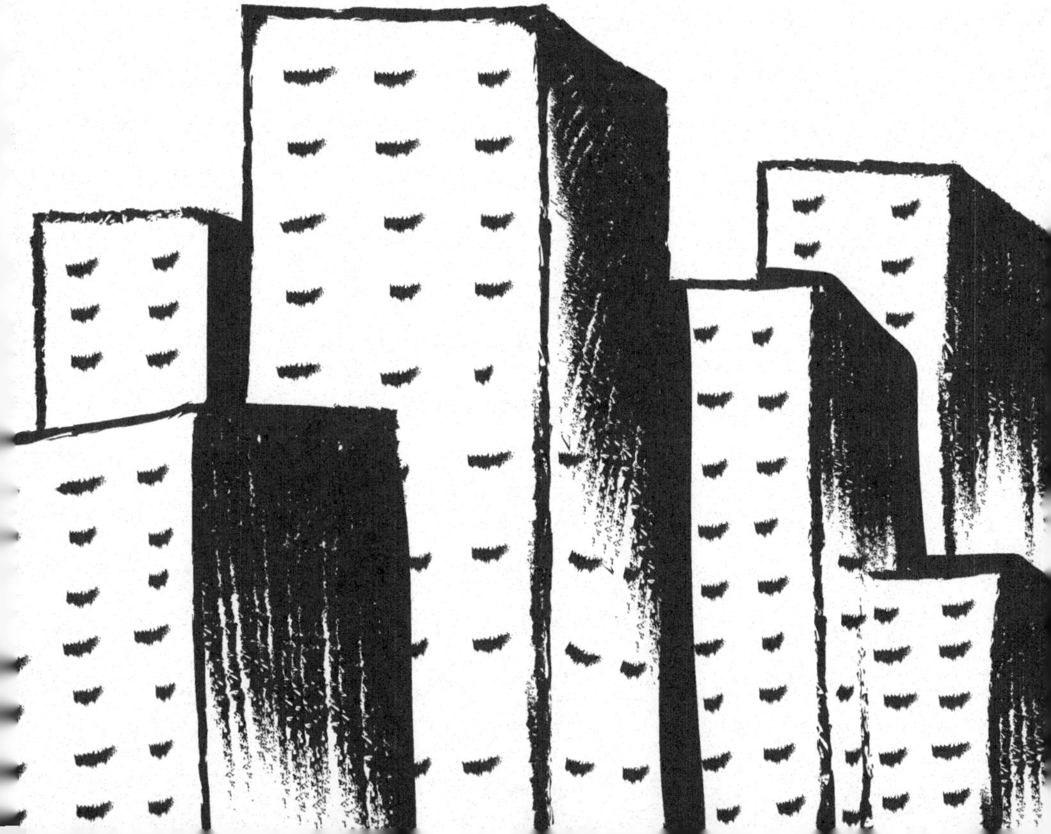

Back to the Future

I looked up. A blue sky, with a few fleecy clouds. In the distance, the sound of traffic—truck horns and car horns competing furiously with each other. I was in my swimming trunks again, the waterproof watch on my wrist. Was this yesterday or tomorrow? Everything seemed just as it had been.

I wasn't sure how I was going to deal with this. I didn't know how long I had been away, or how my parents had handled my absence. Would they believe me? Did *I* believe me? I unclenched my fist to check for the time crystal, which I had held on to so tightly, but of course it had disappeared. No longer whispering and throbbing in my palm, it was probably lying at the bottom of the lake, waiting for the next victim to be transported to some alien time.

'Monal!' Our group master, Mr Sushil's high-pitched voice rang through the air. 'MOE-NAAL!'

I was missing Ghatotkacha already.

'Hoopoe,' he continued, at his military best. 'Hoo-Poooe! Bulbul . . . BOOL-BOOL!'

Scrambling out of the water, I noticed how dirty it was, how unlike the clear lake-water on that other shore. 'Here I am, Mr Sushil! Chintamani from Bulbul.'

He looked at me without any particular interest. 'Oh,' he said. 'Where are the other boys?'

'I-I don't know, sir,' I replied.

'Return to camp!' he commanded and wandered off, still bellowing, 'MOE-NAAAL! HOO-POOOE!'

So I made my way to camp, still more than a little puzzled. Mr Sushil seemed not to have noticed or registered that I had disappeared. *How bizarre!* Feeling a bit wobbly and giddy, I walked up the slope to the field where the tents were pitched.

Bulbul, 2C—that was mine. I shared it with Gopal Gandhi and Jugnu Kishore—both nice boys, not from my school, though. When I entered, they weren't in the tent. In fact, one of the cots had been removed, and only two lay side by side. My mind still racing, I pulled out a tracksuit from my bag and changed before slipping into bed. And suddenly a strange tiredness ran through my body, a wave of utter exhaustion. Time-travel jet lag had caught up with me at last. I was out like a light.

What felt like minutes later, I awoke to find myself shaking and shivering, completely drenched in sweat and blinded by white light. Mr Sushil was shining a torch in my face. He had his stubby fingers around my eyes, as if he was trying to prise

them open.

'He's alive,' I heard him say. 'Thank God, he's alive!'

I followed the beam of torchlight and saw Gopal Gandhi's face—he was sitting cross-legged on his cot and weeping hysterically. Then I blanked out again.

No dreams, no nightmares, no memories, just darkness. When I opened my eyes next, I was in Gurgaon. I was home, in my room, my familiar-unfamiliar room, with its slightly tattered posters and the laptop on a slab by the window that looked out at the traffic below and the tall buildings around. The poster of Bhaichung Bhutia by the door. Another, of Big M—Maradona—in his blue striped T-shirt. These things told me I was home again, in Block A27 of Epic Apartments.

And then there was my mother, looking wildly anxious, coaxing me back into bed when I tried to sit up. 'Beta, you must rest,' she said, repeating herself a few times. 'You *must* rest, beta.' And then, 'The doctors said you must rest!'

My mouth felt dry and my head reeled from having got up from bed too fast. 'Where's Papa?' I asked, and, as if on cue, he materialized.

'Are you feeling better now?' he asked in a causal, trying-not-to-sound-worried voice as he put his arms around Mum. Had they patched up?

'We were worried about you,' he went on. 'The doctors couldn't diagnose anything . . . But you seem fine now.'

I wondered how to begin my story, about where I had been and what had happened. I figured that none of it sounded very convincing. 'I had a strange experience,' I said finally, in a voice that was more casual than my story demanded. 'I was swimming in the lake—in Sat Tal Lake—and I went . . . went back in time. To the days of the Mahabharata. There, I met Ghatotkacha, Lord Bhimasena's son. And Hidimbi . . . Hidimbi Ma. They were very kind to me. And then Dhumavati sent me back. To these times.'

My parents looked at each other concernedly. 'It's the antibiotics,' my mother declared. 'They have made him delirious!'

Papa ignored her. 'Fascinating . . .' he said, his voice full of polite interest. 'You must tell me all about it. But perhaps we can persuade you to eat something first?'

I realized I *was* hungry. Very, very hungry. 'I want an omelette,' I demanded. 'A masala cheese omelette.' My mother rushed towards the kitchen without a word. 'And some toast, and orange juice,' I called after her departing figure, '. . . and chocolate milkshake!'

Well, I couldn't eat that much, but, boy, did I try. Then I lay back in bed again, exhausted by all the activity.

'Hidimbi Ma would make me the most amazing stew,' I said, trying to keep the conversation going.

I sensed them exchanging some more alarmed looks. 'What a bewitching dream, beta,' my mother said brightly, stroking my hair.

'But it wasn't a dream!' I protested, pounding the mattress with my fist. 'It really happened.' Then I gave up. The grown-ups were never going to buy it. Besides, I didn't have any proof—I hadn't even gone missing in earth-time. Present-day time. Kali yuga time. *Back to the Kali yuga*, I told myself consolingly.

'Shh, it was just a nightmare,' my mother said soothingly. 'You were talking about it in your sleep—something about Dwarka, and a parrot?'

'It was a cockatoo,' I explained. 'In Princess Vatsala's palace . . . We . . .' Then, beginning to feeling overpoweringly sleepy again, I dozed right off.

I was back in the forest, among the sal trees, and the sun was about to set. Ghatotkacha was beside me.

'So you are home again, Chintu Pintu,' he said in his special, gentle voice. 'Back in your own time! Don't worry, you are just jet-lagged. And remember, I'm there—just around the corner—if you need me. Whenever.'

Then the stars shone bright in the now inky sky and I could see the Milky Way above me and feel the time crystal snug in my fist. When I awoke, I found I was alone in my room. I felt normal again, though, if 'normal' is the word I'm looking for. I was back to point one, square one, whatever. *Home again*, I told myself over and over. In my own time and place.

I knew, in my heart and my mind and my vivid memory, that I had indeed travelled through some freak episode into a moment deep in the past. I had met Ghatotkacha and could still feel the warm glow of our friendship. But had this really 'happened'? Do *dreams* 'happen'? I didn't seem to have missed out on earth-time, so how could I have travelled into the past? If Ma Dhumavati had sent me back precisely where and when I had got lost in a time warp, did that trip into the past still count as 'real'?

Over the next couple of days, I figured that there were two ways of looking at it: I could either rationalize my encounter as a delusion, maybe cherish it as a precious fantasy. Or I could continue to remember those times, stand by my experience and convince the world that it had happened. And that I was mad, insane, fit to be put away.

Till I landed on a third way: I could continue to believe what I knew was true and 'real', but keep it to myself. I didn't need to share what had now become so much a part of me—and hold it up to ridicule. I could keep quiet and hug my memories in private, perhaps share them when the time was right, with someone who might believe me and what I had to share. The more I thought about it, the more I decided on this course of action. Then, one day, something really strange happened.

The doctors hadn't really been able to diagnose my condition in the first few days of my return. I had had a high temperature and had been raving, but apparently there was also something about my pulse rate and metabolism that confused them. I know now that I was suffering from the trauma of time travel, the peculiar jet lag of travelling across millennia. The specialists then, however, had no reason to suspect this, and had come up with all sorts of possible diseases, including Japanese encephalitis. Finally, it had been our family GP, Dr Ahuja, who had come up with the sensible solution that I continue to rest, and let time and nature heal me.

And indeed I had begun to feel better in the coming weeks. I had also started to sprout the very first signs of a moustache on my upper lip, and this pleased me no end. *Now if only I would grow taller*, I'd continued to wish. It's no fun being short. Before my Dwapara yuga adventure, I would console myself by checking out the heights of famous players. Bhaichung Bhutia—the greatest striker ever—was all of 5 feet 8 inches. Levi Porter: 5 feet 3 inches. The Brazilian Madson Caridade, at 5 feet 3 inches again. There had to be others, I believed. It was consoling to know that inches weren't everything.

So, that day, as I was admiring the tender growth above my lips for the umpteenth time, my glance fell on my ears, usually covered by my hair. They looked different somehow.

My ears were all scrunched-up and wrinkled!

I had seen ears like that before! The rakshasas in Dwarka posing as cloth merchants had ears like that. When Ghatotkacha had transformed into the beautiful princess Vatsala, he had ears like that.

He had explained it to me. 'The ears are the most difficult,' he had said. 'Always watch out for the ears!'

Here, at last, was proof that it had all happened—that I had been morphed and projected back to the future, with the help of Ma Dhumavati's mystical powers and Lord Kubera's time crystal.

Then I took a deep breath. It proved to *me* that I was not hallucinating, but it wasn't really proof, was it? If I told them, the specialists would drive me crazy with their tests and their guesses at why my ears had become wrinkled. And what would I tell them, anyway? 'It happens to rakshasas too when they morph into humans.' Convincing?

Nope.

So I decided, once again, to keep things to myself—to grow my hair a little longer and keep my ears out of sight of inquisitive adults. And yet, every time I saw my crumpled ears, I felt happy, even reassured. It had happened. I was not a nutter!

Life was settling down, and I was getting used to the routine of school and home and parents who were together again, no longer talking about divorce. And then there was football. The excitement of a goal. The comfort of the game. At night, sometimes, I would get strange and vivid dreams, though, and when I awoke, I would be left wondering if I was in this world or the one I had left behind.

One dream returned night after night. Ghatotkacha, on the streets of Gurgaon, with the traffic milling around. He kicks a football in the middle of all that chaos—it hurtles towards me, a tight circle of coiled, twined snakes with hissing fangs . . . before I'd awaken in a cold sweat.

A New Friend

I overheard my mother on the phone one evening. She seemed very upset. 'I can't believe it!' she was saying. 'I just can't believe it. You must be brave . . . We must all be brave.' And she burst into tears.

'What happened?' I asked anxiously, but she wouldn't reply. After much coaxing, the details of the phone call were revealed to me.

My cousin Karuna, who was a little older than me, studied in a boarding school in Nainital. She was an orphan, her parents having died in a car crash when she was little. Her mother and mine had been childhood friends as well as cousins. Her father's elder sister, Paroma Didi, had adopted her after that, bringing her up like her own child.

Well, life had fallen apart for Karuna a second time three weeks ago. Paroma Didi had passed away in a road accident as she and Karuna had been driving together to Delhi for a dental appointment. It had been a long weekend, and Paroma Didi had taken leave from Karuna's school so the girl could see a famous dentist in Vasant Vihar to fix her slightly crooked teeth.

Now Karuna was orphaned all over again. She had fractured both her legs and hurt her back as well. She and the already deceased Paroma Didi had been rushed to a nearby hospital. Their car had collided with that of a well-known television star, who had been speeding and tried to run away after the accident. The public stopped him, and now he was in jail. Didi's relatives had organized the funeral and Karuna had been discharged from hospital. And now she was going to come stay with us until she recovered.

It was shocking. It was tragic. It was unfair. How could life be so cruel? I began sobbing as well, and Mum had to console me, while my father told us we had to be strong and courageous for Karuna's sake. She was going to stay in my room—my parents had fixed up a hospital-type bed in there, one with levers, so she could sit up or put her  legs up, or whatever—and I was to move to the couch in the small study. So I packed some clothes in a suitcase as we wanted her to rest and not be disturbed by my darting in and out of the room.

Later that evening, Karuna arrived in an ambulance and then came up in the lift in a wheelchair, her legs all plastered up. She looked quite composed, I thought, though her face was pale and she had ashen shadows under her eyes. They welled up when she saw my mother, but she smiled through the tears.

'Thank you for having me, Aunty Anuja. I needed to be with family right now,' she said to Mum before turning her head to look at me. 'And Chintamani is always such good company.'

She had called me Chintamani, not Chintu Pintu. She had been through pain and tragedy, and she was smiling, or trying to smile, and being thoughtful. I was impressed.

I kept out of her way at first, thinking she might want to be left alone. She reminded me of a princess in a fairy tale, imprisoned in a tower. I saw that she was trying to be normal, but there was a sort of silent sorrow in that room. Unshed tears and anguish. Eventually, I would drop in to chat with her about this and that. One day, after returning from an exhausting game, I even tried to explain football to Karuna, only to realize that she knew more than me. Really.

'We had a football team in school in Nainital,' she explained, an amused smile on her face. 'Although our coach would call it soccer.' Then her face darkened and her eyes became misty with tears. 'Of course, I may never be able to play again,' she continued, 'after . . . after the accident'.

Life is tough, we know it is. And people die, but it seemed to have been exceptionally cruel to my poor cousin. I took to hanging around in my—her—room more and more, not saying much, just being there. My mother had got Karuna a pile of magazines and comic books, and I perused the former enthusiastically. I actually love all teen magazines—all those 'bare make-up', 'matt vs gloss', 'summer fresh' sort of silly articles. I find them really funny, if you get what I mean.

So, there I was, whistling coolly as I made my way through an article called 'Dieter's Delight', when I was interrupted.

'Are you reading a girly magazine, Chintamani?' Karuna asked suspiciously.

'Yup,' I replied. 'And you can read *Mechanics Today*, if you want. Or *Electronics Now.*' It's a free world!

She waved the Amar Chitra Katha comic book she was reading. 'I'm reading about the Pandavas, thank you,' she said. 'The sons of the Pandavas, actually. About Ghatotkacha.'

A peculiar, cold shiver ran down my back and my hair stood on end when I heard her say that. I snatched the comic book from her hand and began feverishly leafing through it. The Pandavas! I had met them, all except Arjuna. And my friend Ghatotkacha. He looked nothing like the ugly, hairy monster the illustrator had made him out to be! It made me livid.

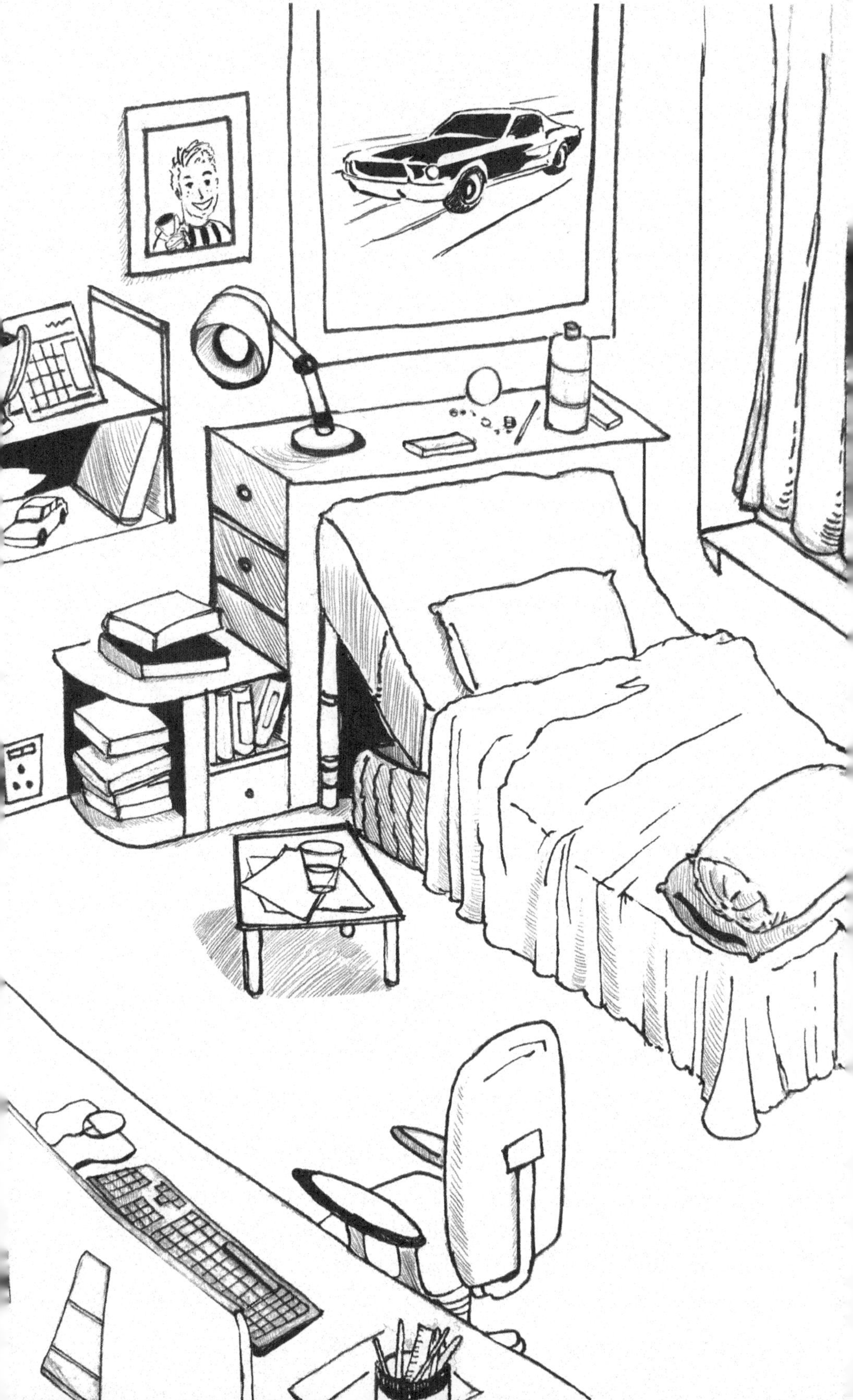

'That's NOT what he looked like!' I said out loud. There was something in my voice that made her sit up promptly, even though she was in a hospital bed with her legs in plaster.

'Chintu!' she exclaimed. 'Chintu Pintu, what's wrong? Why are you so upset?'

I pointed to the comic book. 'That's *not* what Ghatotkacha looked like,' I said again, a quiet anger coursing through my words. 'Ghatotkacha is a very nice guy, and very handsome.'

'Really?' Karuna replied. 'And I suppose you've met him? Ghatotkacha is your best buddy, huh?'

'As a matter of fact, he is,' I shot back, something snapping inside me. 'You are the first and probably the only person who will ever hear this story. So listen carefully. Suspend disbelief. And *don't* laugh.'

Then I pulled back the hair from around my ears. 'Do you see this?' I said. 'Do you see my ears? There is a reason why they are like that. We will come to that in the end, when we return to the present. But first, you must listen. *Carefully.*'

And she did. Karuna's eyes did not mock me, neither did she seem to think I had gone mad. She listened, took it all in with the resigned patience of someone who, having encountered the very worst the world can offer, was no longer surprised by life's surprises.

I was still in the beginning of my story, telling her of how I had been swimming in Sat Tal Lake and of the sofa-shaped rocks at the bottom and of suddenly arriving at what was the same place but another time. I was telling her of these things when she put her finger to her lips.

'Shush,' she said. 'Chintamani, can you stop for a moment? I want to feel your ears.'

Well, what could I say? I leaned forward and she touched my ears, like a doctor almost, an ENT specialist. I actually liked having my ears stroked, I realized, no one had ever done that before. Then she bent forward and stared at them intently.

'Hold on,' she said, and took a picture with her iPhone, one of each ear. And 'Carry on!' when she was done. 'Sorry to have interrupted you.'

Just then, my mother walked in.

'What are you two gabbing about?' she inquired with the forced cheerfulness with which older people sometimes talk to young adults they consider 'children'.

'Nothing much,' I mumbled casually. 'This and that.' And so we suspended my story that afternoon.

But over the next week, I told Karuna all about my adventures. They sounded hardly believable when I recounted them, even to me. But telling her about those days brought them alive again. I was so lost in remembering, reliving that strange and magical interlude that I didn't really care if *she* believed me or not.

When I told her about the whistling—how *I* had taught the mighty Ghatotkacha to whistle—she implored, 'Teach me! Please, Chintu Pintu . . .'

And so I did. Before I knew it, we were whistling to each other like a pair of cockatoos.

I told her of the cockatoo as well, the one in Princess Vatsala's palace. She was fascinated by my descriptions of Dwarka— the shining spires, the domes, the silver- and crystal-encrusted buildings.

'Really?' she asked, her eyes gleaming. 'Maybe we could go back together sometime—just you and me.' Karuna was suddenly serious. I could see a glistening tear form in the corner of her eye.

I didn't say anything. Pretended I hadn't noticed anything.

She swallowed her tears, and acted as though she had just been sniffing very hard. Then she cleared her throat. 'If—if we can go back in time, then the past still exists. That means there is no such thing as death, you know? That means that my parents are . . . not dead. They are alive in the past, at some time, somewhere. And Paroma Didi too—she is alive, will stay alive, at some time, somewhere.'

'That sounds logical,' I replied, 'and likely.' I wanted desperately to reassure her, to make her happy. 'All time is eternally present,' I went on consolingly. I didn't really know what that meant, but it sounded right. And true.

In answer, she began whistling—the same tune that I had taught Ghatotkacha and which she had only just learnt. I whistled it back to her. We looked at each other, pleased with ourselves. Now we were only looking at each other, and neither of us was whistling.

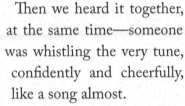

Then we heard it together, at the same time—someone was whistling the very tune, confidently and cheerfully, like a song almost.

We turned around in shock and expectation. The strain seemed to be coming from the window. My friend Ghatotkacha! I thought I saw him, his face reflected in the windowpane. And then he was gone.

The Greatest
Story Ever Told

Karuna was laid up in bed for almost a month, and I was caught up with homework and football practice and things like that. Exam time was fast approaching. But we managed to spend our evenings together. Sometimes we would watch television. The mythological serials were fun, and of special interest if they depicted episodes from the Mahabharata.

'That's *so* not what it was like,' I would explain passionately, and Karuna would rib me saying I should get an 'MMBS' degree—a 'Master of Mahabharata Studies'!

As I watched the dramatic scenes on TV with Karuna, I realized that, apart from having met four of the five Pandavas, I knew very little about the Mahabharata. I had heard Hidimbi Ma's tales of her husband, Lord Bhimasena, met Abhimanyu and Princess Vatsala, admired Draupadi and got a glimpse of the arrogant and handsome Duryodhana. And then, of course, there was Ghatotkacha, my beloved friend Ghatotkacha. But no one else around me seemed to have heard of him much, nor did he ever seem to appear onscreen.

Like most people I know, I had never actually read the Mahabharata. I remembered the story in bits and snatches, from here and there—from films and now television and some comic books earlier. And from the stories my grandmother, Mum's mother, used to tell me. I decided I needed to know more about the great old epic first-hand. My mother had given me *The Puffin Mahabharata* back on my eleventh birthday and had urged me to read it. 'It's the greatest story ever told,' she had said. Of course, I hadn't taken her advice and it had stood in a corner of my bookshelf for over two years.

Now I brought it down and examined it. It was still new and shiny, though a bit dusty. A striking yellow jacket, with an archer poised with his bow and arrow. *The Puffin Mahabharata* by Namita Gokhale. I turned the cover.

A long, long time ago, in the ancient lands of India, known in those days as Bharatvarsha, a family quarrel grew into a bloody war. There had been wars before, and there have been wars since, but that mighty battle between warring cousins of the Kuru clan has become a part of the mythology and history of India. Told and retold a million times, the story of the Mahabharata is about defeat as well as victory, humility as much as courage. It is the greatest story ever told.

There are four cycles of time that rule our universe, which are known in Sanskrit as the four yugas. These are the Satya, the Treta, the Dwapara and the Kali yugas. The Mahabharata war was fought at the very end of the Dwapara yuga. And as the heroic Pandavas began their last journey, to find their place in heaven or in hell, the Kali yuga of our present, mortal times began.

It was almost three thousand years ago, in what is now northern India, that the Kuru kingdom flourished by the banks of the river Yamuna. It was here, in the city of Hastinapura and in nearby Kurukshetra, that the great battle was fought. The kings and princes who are the heroes of the tale were all descendants of King Bharata, and so it is known today as the Mahabharata. However, in the beginning it had a simple title and was known only as the 'Jaya', the song of victory.

Three thousand years ago! So that's how long back I had travelled. I flipped through the book impatiently. It was gripping stuff, I admit, but I was hunting for mentions of my giant friend. I read about the river goddess Ganga, who had come down to earth in human form and was beautiful beyond belief. And about how King Santanu of Hastinapura, ancestor of the Kauravas and the Pandavas, saw Ganga and instantly fell in love with her.

'Marry me and be my queen,' he pleaded.

But Ganga was an immortal and understandably reluctant to marry a mortal, even though he happened to be a king. She set some stiff conditions for him, and he was never, ever to question her about anything she might do. And so they got married, but each time Ganga had a child, she killed it by drowning the innocent babe in the river. Santanu stopped her when she was about to cast their eighth child into the water. She explained the complex reason for her actions to the bewildered king, and then left with their child.

Later, Santanu was reunited with his son Devavrata, who was anointed as his heir. Then Santanu fell in love again, this time with Satyawati, and he wanted to make her his queen. But Satyawati would agree only on the condition that her children alone would inherit Santanu's kingdom. Hearing this, the young prince Devavrata nobly renounced his claim to the throne. To Uparichara, Satyawati's father, he said:

> I will do anything for my father's happiness. I give you my word that I shall never aspire to inherit the throne or the kingdom. I renounce all my rights as my father's eldest son to be his heir apparent, if that can persuade you to let your daughter marry my father.

I thought about this a bit. Would I do this for my father? Would my father ever expect it of me? Highly unlikely, and of course, there was no kingdom for me or anyone else to inherit. Those times were different, I reflected. Ghatotkacha too was the firstborn son of Bhima but, even though the Pandavas had been in exile then, nobody—his own father included—seemed to bother much about him. Was it because Ghatotkacha was half-rakshasa? Either way, in our times, we sure expected more of our dads. While I still puzzled to make sense of this, the story moved on.

Ah, this bit! So I knew the plot from here on, sort of. Dhritarashtra, who was born blind, ascended the throne when Pandu, his cousin, was cursed by a sage and decided to retire to the forest. Dhritarashtra's wife, Gandhari, blindfolded herself all her life so she could share her husband's blindness, giving birth to a hundred sons, the Kauravas, and a daughter, Dushala. Meanwhile, Pandu's wives, Kunti and Madri, gave birth to the five Pandava brothers—Yudhishthira, Bhima, Arjuna, Nakula and Sahadeva—while living in retreat in the forest. And some time after that, well, a winding game of thrones began—the warring cousins, the hundred Kauravas and the five Pandavas, battled to the end for the kingdom.

Let me tell you, as strange as it felt to read about the key characters in the Mahabharata—I mean, I had been there, seen them, met them—for the next few days, my eyes scanned the pages for who else but Ghatotkacha. My frustrations were somewhat quelled when Karuna joined me in my attempt, and the two of us would go through the book together, sometimes reading out bits to each other.

At last, one evening, we got to the part where the Pandavas were wandering in the forests after escaping from the wax palace, where their cruel cousins had attempted to burn them alive. It was Karuna's turn to read the chapter out loud. 'Hidimb and Hidimbi,' she began.

Suddenly my mind took me back to the shock I had felt when Hidimbi Ma had explained the ingredients that went into a traditional rakshasa stew and how she had given up on human flesh after she had met Lord Bhimasena and married him. That enormous pot, with curling flames licking its sides, and the delicious smells wafting through the hut as Ghatotkacha and I hungrily awaited our dinner—all these things came alive for me when Karuna began reading aloud from the pages.

And then it wasn't Karuna any more, but Hidimbi herself who was telling me the story! I couldn't understand if it was old-fashioned rakshasa technology or my hyperactive imagination. Or was it that stories have different frequencies, and we can enter them differently when they already exist in our experience and our imagination? So the day when Hidimbi Ma had first met Bhima had come alive for me in her gravelly voice, with that hint of laughter in it, in Karuna's telling and in my memory.

'Chintu Pintu, let me tell you how it all really happened,' she was saying. 'My brother, Hidimb, was sitting on the highest branch of the tallest deodar tree on the hill, watching out for trouble and treats. I was on another branch nearby, humming a rakshasa song as I combed my hair, when "Look down, sister!" he exclaimed. And I did. There were five men asleep on the grass, their bows and arrows and maces guarded in their arms, while their gentle snores broke the silence. And there was a woman curled up beside them—Kunti, who was to become my mother-in-law.

'My brother, Hidimb, was a lazy one, and mean and spiteful too, when he was in one of his moods. "Get them for me, sister," he snarled. "Fetch them and roast them, and we shall have a feast tonight. Stupid mortals, venturing into my forest to become rakshasa stew!"

'"It's my forest too, brother!" I pointed out. "And I'm not very hungry. We had a feast just yesterday, and the pot is full of leftovers. Let them be, and give them safe passage."

'Hidimb flew into one of his rages when he heard my response. "You are just a stupid girl-rakshasa!" he screamed. "Do as you are told and get them for me!"

'Well, there was not much point in arguing with him, so I decided to go down and take a look at the sleeping humans. They lay languorously on the grass, and I could see, even then, that these were no ordinary mortals. They were incredibly handsome, each and all of them, with a nobility and strength I had never ever seen before. One of them turned over, still clutching his mace, and the muscles in his chest rippled like the waves in a pond. And I fell in love with him, in that moment and forever. I knew this was where my heart belonged, where my duty lay, where my future rested. That's the thing about love, Chintu Pintu—when it finds you, everything else stops to matter! Some day, little one, some day, you too will fall in love, and you too will understand what Hidimbi Ma was going on about!'

And then I could hear Karuna's voice again, her face buried in the book.

When Hidimbi saw the sleeping Bhima, with his enormous muscular body, lean hips and wrestler's thighs, she fell instantly in love with him. While Hidimbi was beautiful by demon standards, she knew that this would not appeal to human eyes. She used her rakshasi powers to transform herself into the most beautiful maiden possible. She now had large, expressive eyes, with thick eyelashes that she batted incessantly, and an enchanting dimpled smile.

I knew the story from here—Hidimbi Ma had told it to me on those long, dark nights in the forest a zillion years ago. She had told me that only Bhima had existed for her after that, and that she had given up on everything she knew—the rakshasa life she had grown up in, all the habits and customs that were so much a part of her, even her brother, the demon Hidimb, whom she loved—to become a loyal daughter-in-law to Kunti and a devoted bride to the Pandava Bhima. She was a tough lady and a courageous one, I reflected, as Karuna went on.

Soon their time in Salivahana was up. Kunti and her sons wept many tears at the prospect of leaving Ghatotkacha behind, with only Hidimbi to look after him. But the brave rakshasi kept her word and did not weep a single tear, although her heart was broken at the prospect of being parted from her beloved Bhima.

'Look after our son,' Bhima told her. 'I shall always be with you in my thoughts. Whenever you need me, just think of me and I will arrive by your side.' Yudhishthira held Ghatotkacha in his arms and blessed him, and then it was time for them to begin their wanderings again.

So there he was, my friend, at last finding his place in the story. I was glad his uncle Yudhishthira had watched out for him. And I thought of Hidimbi Ma, of her generosity, her laughter, the fragrance that surrounded and followed her.

We shut the book for the day and the story continued the next morning, Karuna and I trading places as before—but there was no sign of Ghatotkacha for pages and pages after, which were devoted to the Pandavas and the Kauravas being caught up in a battle on the fields of Kurukshetra to put an end to their lifelong hostility.

The military terms and formations fascinated me, though. I learnt that an *akshauhini* was an army division consisting of 21,870 chariots, the same number of elephants, 65,610 horses and 1,09,350 footmen. The battle formations were really imaginative too. There was the *krauncha*, where the soldiers were gathered in the shape of a bird; the *padavyuh*, where the army was arranged in the form of a full-blown lotus; the *suchimukhavyuh*, where the standing soldiers tapered into a needle point, where there was maximum protection, and so on.

And then there was the *chakravyuh*. Karuna read aloud the chapter in which it made its formidable appearance. I can still remember the moment—it was late afternoon, and the sounds of distant traffic spilled into my room. Car horns, trucks, the wail of an ambulance siren.

I was excited at first, to think of my friend's handsome cousin Abhimanyu, so invincible in battle. Then, as the tale unravelled, I began shivering with fear and anticipation. And in my cousin's quiet voice opened up another dimension in which I could see the story unfolding through Abhimanyu's own eyes. I could imagine the swirling dust and the smell of blood and the cries of battle and the sharp clangs of swords and shields and the thuds of iron maces. I was there with him, with bold Abhimanyu, as he battled for his father, Arjuna, being too young to know all that he should have known but too brave not to have paid the price of courage.

> Young Abhimanyu was trapped in a chakravyuh he could not escape, and confronted with the brutality and treachery of his enemies. Tired and fatigued, he slumped to the ground. Dusasana's son rushed at him with a mace and killed the fallen hero. Abhimanyu's last thought was regret that Arjuna had not been there to see him fight his first and last battle.

Karuna's voice wavered and I could sense the sob that she gulped and swallowed as she stopped reading. We sat together in silence for a while.

Abhimanyu, the stately prince in love with the beautiful princess Vatsala. It was simply heartbreaking. What was the point of war? Why did people continue to fight? Didn't they learn? *Couldn't* they learn? Before I knew it, I was tearing up beyond control and Karuna eyed me with concern. She got up slowly, wincing with pain, and walked over to where I was sitting. Without a word, she hugged me. She smelled of shampoo and chewing gum.

'Let's not read any more,' I said. For I was already afraid of what I knew might, *would*, happen.

I was really morose for the next few days. School, football practice, the time I spent with Karuna—these things happened in a well-rehearsed routine. But it was as though a heavy weight had descended on my head, and my heart. Meanwhile, Karuna's plaster was due to be removed soon. There was a spell of holidays, and then she would be back in her boarding school in Nainital.

My mother noticed that I was quieter than usual, but she tactfully avoided asking me outright. 'Are you well, Chintu Pintu?' she said worriedly. 'I hope you aren't coming down with a virus or something.'

'I'm well, Mum,' I replied. 'And please don't call me Chintu Pintu. I'm Chintamani. That's the name—the strange, inexplicably long name—you gave me. So call me Chintamani.'

'You've been reading the Mahabharata,' she persisted. 'Are you enjoying it?'

'It's for a school project,' I answered non-committally.

There is just a part of my life my parents will probably never know nor understand, even if I tell them.

Hours of Magical Dreaming

One night, when I couldn't sleep, I picked up the book and read ahead by myself. I had dozed off around midnight only to awake just as dawn was breaking. Now I returned to the dog-eared page, the words illuminated by the orange patch of sky outside my window.

The chapter was titled 'Ghatotkacha'.

> Ghatotkacha, Bhima's son born of the demoness Hidimbi, came from his forest home to assist his father and uncles in battle. He was a young man of heroic strength and power. His war cries sent shivers of fear through the Kaurava camp, and his savage team of rakshasas was almost invincible.

I was once again lost in the words. I could virtually see the ravaged battlefield from my mighty friend's point of view. The gentle giant, the firstborn son of the Pandavas, had been unswerving in his love and loyalty to his family, even if they didn't have much use for him until and unless his awesome strength was needed.

> Ghatotkacha's first memorable encounter was with Ashwathama. Bhima's son used the power of magical delusion to confuse his

enemy, but Ashwathama countered him with his vast armoury of divine *astras*.

The powers of rakshasas increase in the dark of night. Breaking all the rules of warfare, the battle between Ghatotkacha and Ashwathama continued late into the hours of magical darkness.

Karna came to the rescue of the Kaurava army. He fought bravely, but his unwavering aim was of no use in the face of Ghatotkacha's powers of illusion. Ghatotkacha would change his form at will and so Karna's arrows could never find their target. When he rained stones on the Kaurava army, Karna countered it with the *yayavyastra*. When he sent out a huge rain cloud that dripped lethal arrows, Karna let loose his *aindrastra*. The Kaurava army was speechless with terror. Karna realized that unless he acted immediately, they might surrender to the Pandavas. He decided to use the Shakti, the weapon given to him by Lord Indra in return for his invincible golden breastplate and earrings. He had reserved the Shakti for his final and decisive encounter with Arjuna, but now he had no option but to employ it to counter Ghatotkacha. The Shakti streaked across the sky at the speed of lightning, piercing the cloak of illusion with which Ghatotkacha defended himself. Bhima's son fell to earth, but even as he died he summoned his magical powers one last time. His body swelled and grew until it was an enormous, heavy mass, and as it landed on the Kaurava army, it destroyed one entire akshauhini with the impact of its fall.

I could picture it all painfully vividly. The dark night streaked with the lightning movements of the magical astras. At the heart of it, patient Ghatotkacha, with his mastery of illusions, and impatient Karna. I knew how Ghatotkacha might have felt, faced with his death. He must have resolved to do his best even then, at the end, when all was lost. He must have gathered his strength and

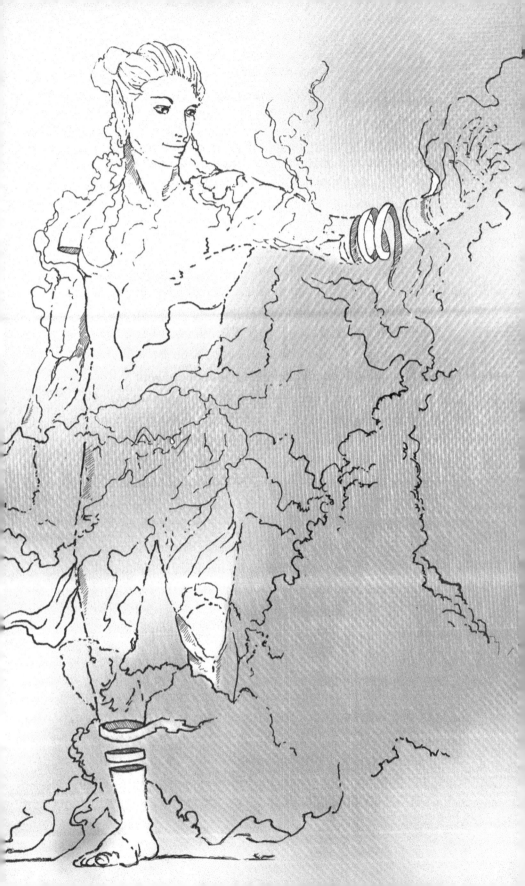

summoned his magical powers to grow and expand his body, to fight that final battle even as he died, devoting his last breaths to his father and the Pandavas. I continued reading, even though my mind was racing and my eyes were blurred with tears.

Bhima felt his heart would break. The price of the war was higher than what even this bravest of warriors could bear. His beloved firstborn son, Ghatotkacha, was dead. Even as Bhima grieved, Krishna smiled an inscrutable smile. He knew, now that Karna had used the Shakti, his favourite cousin Arjuna was safe.

Karna, too, was depressed and disheartened. His fate was sealed. The desperate measures that had dictated the premature use of his ultimate weapon had spelt out his own doom.

It was one of the shortest chapters in the book. *That* upset me . . . it seriously upset me. It was as though he didn't deserve any more. And the illustration took up most of the two pages with the image of an ugly, bloated demon. That wasn't how I knew him, remembered him.

So this was how my gentle giant friend had died. In desperation, in hope, I recalled his rough, kind face, the large ears, the jewel on his forehead. What was it he had said?

I could still hear his words, like he were speaking to me here, now.

'Remember, nothing ever dies. Look at the moon—you would think it has died, it has disappeared . . . but it waxes and wanes and waxes again. You might think it has died, but it returns.'

The memory of Ghatotkacha's words gave me comfort; but the thought of his death on the battlefield of Kurukshetra and the memory of his strength, his courage, even in the end, left me devastated.

The days followed in a haze, the mysterious fever having reappeared. I was delirious again and losing weight rapidly. My parents were crazed with worry. They thought my recent— undiagnosed—disease had resurfaced. Which, in a way, was what I now suppose had happened.

I was taken like a sack of potatoes to the doctor. I had an MRI and a CAT scan, and all sorts of blood tests. I remember spending two nights in hospital. Then one day, I was better, and the next day, totally fine again. My mother called a priest, an old-fashioned pandit, and she had a havan performed at home. The living room was smoky and smelled of incense, and there were marigold flowers everywhere.

Once I was back to my usual self, I remembered that Karuna was to return to school in a few days. She had recovered too, though I knew my illness had shaken her up, badly. I could see it in the way she would look at me when she didn't know that I was watching her watching me.

That evening, after the puja was long over, I was sitting in her room—my old room, soon to be mine again. Reassured, my parents had left for a cocktail party earlier. It was in south Delhi somewhere, and I suspected it was going to be a late night. They were so very relieved that I was well again, and I was happy for them too, as though I were the parent.

Anyway, Karuna and I were sort of aimlessly letting the evening flow by. Our friendship had reached the stage where we didn't really need speak to each other, and a shrug or a lifted eyebrow was enough to convey what we were thinking. I mean, when we absolutely needed to talk, we could bare our hearts to each other, but we didn't have to do it all the time.

Suddenly, I heard a familiar jaunty whistle and turned to Karuna to see what she was up to. She'd turned to me as well. We were staring at each other quizzically when we heard the tune again. It wasn't either of us.

To my right, though, a massive figure was materializing in the room! I still don't quite know how to describe it: it was like a grainy 3D image assembling itself, like a giant jigsaw puzzle gone berserk. Then there were the huge bare feet, the curly shoulder hair, the enormous jug-shaped ears, the copper-coloured arms. The last bit of him to appear was the brass-and-gold helmet, with the small green jewel mounted on the crest.

Ghatotkacha!

The apparition was crouching slightly to fit into the room, the jewel on the helmet all but scraping the ceiling. Nevertheless, my friend was whistling the same tune I had taught him in our jungle days together. Then he changed his melody, this time a long, mellow, deep note followed by a sharp chirp. It was the tune he had exchanged with the cockatoo in Princess Vatsala's bedchamber in Dwarka. 'I am here,' he announced. 'I am here, Chintu Pintu! Here I am!'

But I couldn't *believe* he was there before me! Was I hallucinating?

Karuna had gone pale with wonder. So she could see him too! Recovering from my astonishment, I introduced them, my two best friends, to each other.

'Ghatotkacha, this is Karuna. And Karuna, this is Ghatotkacha, whom you have heard so much about.' Turning to him, I asked, 'What are you doing *here*? I mean, why . . . *how* are you here?'

A surprising thing was happening even as I spoke. My friend was downsizing, reassembling, until he was of human height. I mean, he was of course much taller than me, and Karuna too, but he didn't have to stoop uncomfortably any more. He was almost at eye level now, the green jewel having left a long scratch on the plaster ceiling. Without answering my fervent question, he settled down in my computer chair and began swivelling around, tentatively at first, then faster and faster like a whirling dervish. I felt giddy looking at him.

'So, this is your room,' he said. 'It's higher than our sal trees up here.'

'It's a high-rise,' I explained. But my mind was on other things. 'I've been reading about the war, Ghatto . . .' I began anxiously. 'I mean, the battle of Kurukshetra. A-and how you . . . you died. You were *so* heroic!'

Then I felt awkward, for it was, after all, an awkward sort of thing to have said.

'Nothing and nobody ever completely dies,' Ghatotkacha replied matter-of-factly. 'I've told you this all those thousands of years ago. Besides, humans live, humans "die", but the rishis and the immortals are different. We rakshasas are different too. We never surrender all our life force. So even though I was eliminated from the battlefield by Karna's most powerful weapon, his Shakti-astra, I could reimagine myself and teleport *that* form here. I was just mighty worried about you, young un, and decided to pay you a visit.' He turned to Karuna. 'But I see you are in good hands,' he said, summoning a most charming smile, 'very good hands indeed!'

'You look the same as ever, Ghatto,' I said. 'You haven't changed at all!' Then I realized that was not a very bright thing to say, considering he had come across hundreds of thousands of years, really.

'You see me as you remember me,' Ghatotkacha answered. 'Time did not allow the hair on my chest to grey, but I had many adventures after you left. I was blessed with a brave and loyal wife, Ahilawati, and two noble sons, Barbarika and Meghavarna. My wife is the daughter of the snake god Bashaka, who rules draped around Lord Shiva's neck. My son Barbarika was sacrificed by Lord Krishna before the great bloodbath at Kurukshetra. And I was sacrificed too, by the deadliest weapon of them all, the Vasavi Shakti, the divine astra of the unfortunate Karna. He killed me, but I call him unfortunate because he killed himself too when he unleashed the Vasavi astra, his last refuge in battle, against me. When he re-entered into battle without the protection of the Shakti, it was ordained that he would be defeated by Arjuna.'

It made my hair stand on end to hear him speak of the events. I shuddered, and tears welled up in my eyes. But Ghatotkacha seemed not to be bothered and simply continued. 'On reflection, I saved my uncle Arjuna's life with my death. Lord Karna—and he was my uncle too, brother to the Pandavas—had saved that last weapon only and only for Lord Arjuna. But it was not to be. Truly, life is a game. Winning and losing are nothing but illusions, for we are the playthings of the gods, however strong we think we may be.'

Something was happening to Ghatotkacha as he sat before us. He was pixelating somehow, like an image on a screen that had been over-enlarged. His voice began wavering and there was an urgency in it, as though he was being torn away.

'I must go now, my friend. It's not easy to transport to another time and place, and to assume a physical dimension there. So this brief visit must end. I must return. Adieu! And until we meet again!'

'No, Ghatto, not yet!' I cried in vain, my voice desperate with sadness.

Joy and wonder, sorrow and regret, and the sheer impossibility of what I—we—were witnessing had left me quite breathless. I turned to Karuna; she was smiling inscrutably and didn't seem surprised or shaken up at all!

'Give me a high five, my friends,' he declared, and even as we raised our arms, he sort of dismantled, disintegrated and, finally, disappeared.

We sat in silence for a long time after that. There was nothing we could say to each other. Karuna and I had shared something together that we could not have—would never—with anyone else. Our lives would be linked forever, somehow. That felt good and right.

'He was . . . I mean, he is a really nice guy,' Karuna said reflectively. I nodded in reply, then walked over to the window to stare at the endless stream of traffic so far below us.

'Chintamani . . .' she continued, 'Chintamani, whose pants are you are wearing? They just reach your calves!'

I looked down and, yes, I *was* too tall for my trousers! I realized I *felt* different . . . that my line of vision had shifted. Karuna got up and quietly stood next to me, and I looked down into her soft brown eyes for the briefest moment.

Well, there it was. Ghatotkacha had worked his magic with that parting high five! I was taller, much taller than I had ever been. I instinctively looked up at the ceiling. A spider was crawling across the roof, where the dent left behind by Ghatotkacha's jewelled brass–gold helmet was there for all to see.

My parents returned home from their party soon after. They looked cheery, and a little woozy.

'You folks still awake?' my father asked. 'Everything okay?'

'Everything okay?' my mother repeated.

'Everything okay!' Karuna and I replied as we beamed at each other.

The Puzzles of Time

This strange, almost unbelievable, encounter, along with my adventures in the Dwapara yuga, transformed me in more ways than I can ever list. I grew taller. I became surprisingly good at my studies. And I became deeply interested in the past and the future, and the nature of that unpredictable creature called time.

To throw some light on the mysteries I had been faced with, first I decided to know as much as I could about Dwarka, the city of which I had such vivid memories. According to the history books, ancient Dwarka had drowned in a flood, been swallowed whole by the sea. But how, why had that terrible calamity occurred?

For that answer, I had to rewind even further. The Mahabharata says that after the Kurukshetra War, Lord Krishna returned to the kingdom of Dwarka, which he ruled together with his brother Balarama. But with the great battle over, peacetime made the clan rough and rowdy. When the sages Vishwamitra and Narada and some other holy men came to Dwarka, the young men of the royal family decided to play a stupid practical joke on them. The prank made the sages really angry, and they cursed the clan for all time to come.

Well, to cut a long story short, bad things began to happen. A guy called Samba, Krishna's son—the one who had performed the stunt by pretending to be a pregnant woman and asking the sages to predict the supposed unborn child's gender—gave birth to an iron rod. Balarama recognized the portents, and had the iron rod pulped and powdered and thrown deep into the sea— the same Arabian Sea I remember so well, as seen from Princess Vatsala's chamber. In the days to come, though, things only got worse. There were brawls and fights and beheadings in the clan. And then the sea rose in a mighty thundering wave and drowned the city altogether.

My hair stood on end when I read about it in *The Puffin Mahabharata*. So that's how the magnificent eight-gated city was lost forever. The ocean had risen like a tower of water and lashed into the turrets and palaces that I had once flown past, held aloft in Ghatotkacha's strong arms.

Its deep roar was like a sigh through the heavens, and the salt water coursed through the streets of Krishna's capital. It submerged the beautiful buildings and palaces, and soon the city had sunk without a trace into the water. Time leaves nothing true, and not a trace remained of the grandeur of Dwarka.

I became increasingly obsessed with Dwarka. Forgetting about homework and football and all the other things that made up my schoolboy life, I started looking up things on the Net. My parents were a bit worried by this sudden information addiction, but I told them it was for a big school project and that seemed to calm them down.

My extensive research taught me that the original city of Dwarka is perhaps 9500 years old, older even than the Egyptian and Mesopotamian civilizations. The scientific angle says that the melting of the ice caps and the end of the ice age, about 8000–10,000 years ago, caused the sea level to rise by almost 400 feet, swallowing the ancient site of Dwarka city. Just like the world-engulfing deluge that launched Noah's Ark, in which the animals walked in two by two.

I even found tons of videos on YouTube, some that speculated on the lost city and others with underwater divers pointing out the ruins of great buildings as evidence. They spoke of Dwarka as the mystic Atlantis of the East. While watching these, my mind returned again and again to the palaces and parks of that wondrous city of crystals and emeralds I had once visited, millennia ago, the city of Ghatotkacha and the mischievous rakshasas, and of the blessed couple Vatsala and Abhimanyu. Despite days of study, that's how I will always remember it.

But do look up the films when you find the time. You will see the carved pillars and the giant blocks of stone buried deep with the other secrets of the sea, like a vague memory. You will see the divers slowly floating around in their gear, as if they were travellers in space. Although when the cameras focus on them from below, their flippers kind of make them look like a giant frog species.

I've decided I want to sign up for one of the underwater expeditions. Perhaps during a gap year after I am through with school. I have promised myself I *will* go there, to that seashore, to those depths. The soonest I can manage, I will learn to dive, to

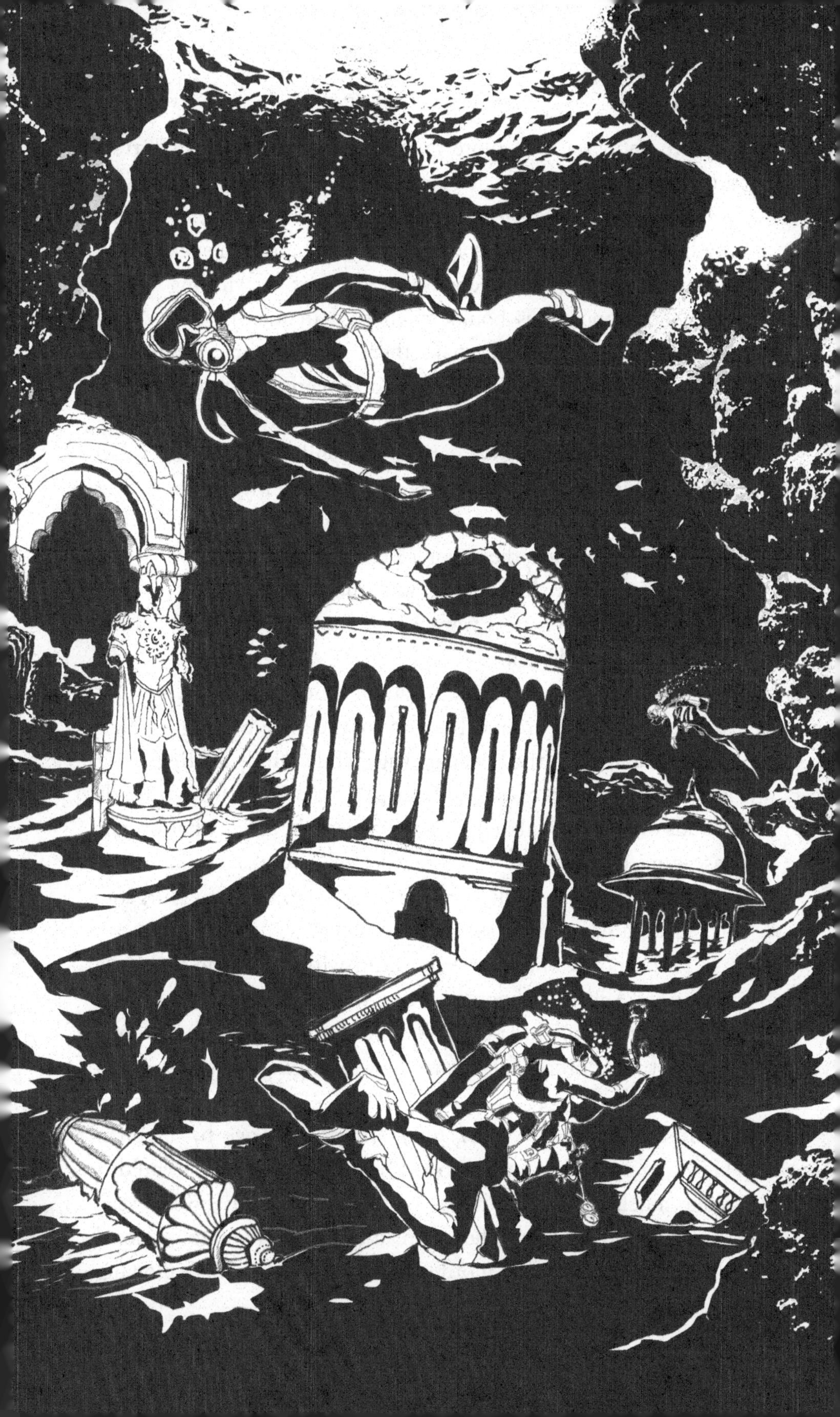

venture undersea, to explore the submerged city with its turrets and castles, now made ancient, fabled, through the passage of time.

Even today, in between dream and nightmare, I recall the day my head had hit against something and I had been sucked into the water, deeper and deeper, into a vortex of whirling waves. And those enormous boulders, covered in mossy-green slime, like giant velvet sofas. Perhaps there are still some mysterious passages to the past in the drowned remains of Dwarka? Who knows? I will go there. I will find out. Some day.

Karuna thought I was getting too philosophical, and I *had* been thinking about these things a lot. I found myself wondering about time, what it is, how it rules our lives. Wasn't I entitled to do that, more than other people? More than anybody I know? I mean, I've personally grappled with the serpent of time—I have been swallowed by a time warp, I have travelled to the days of the Mahabharata and back.

And so I began been reading about time travel. There are a lot of theories floating around, but none of them seem to suggest that one can catapult to the Dwapara yuga while calmly floating along in the placid waters of Sat Tal Lake and practising a backstroke. It sounds even more unlikely that a wizened old lady with grey hair cascading to her waist and a murder of crows surrounding her could transport me back from those long-ago times to Gurgaon, or Gurugram, as it now seems to be called.

Time moves on. Do we move on with it? Or do we move within it? And what happens when we die? These were the sort of thoughts occupying my mind, even as the poster of Maradona stared at me reproachfully from the wall, urging me to go out, to run and play and get on with the game.

Instead, I borrowed *A Brief History of Time* by Stephen Hawking from my father's bookshelf. To be honest, I couldn't make much sense of it, try as I might. Maybe in another year, when I'm older. Or in college. I read this other book too, a novel about the uroboros, the motif of a serpent or dragon swallowing its own tail. Now, that image sort of made sense to me—the serpent of time with its tail in its mouth. I sure felt as though the time-serpent had swallowed me up, deep into the past, and then hissed and spat me out again.

Perhaps quantum physics is also right. I read that our universe is full of wormholes—minute ones, even smaller than atoms, which integrate and disintegrate in the briefest instants. Harnessing and expanding one to a size large enough for humans to travel through could be possible in theory, I suppose. And then I found something about travelling faster than light, which suggested that time travellers dive through a convenient wormhole. A website explained, with a caveat:[1]

> Wormholes are theoretical warps in the fabric of reality that connect two points of space-time by a shorter distance than they are separated by in the larger continuum. Wormholes could connect distant galaxies, separate universes, and even different times. Much like traveling faster than light, however, the practicalities of stable wormhole creation and travel likely make this option impossible.

Karuna and I puzzled over this for a while, struggling to make sense of it. We decided it was a sort of shortcut, really, in simple terms. And then there were the time crystals and the tachyons.

---

[1] 'How to Go Back in Time', *Project: Time Travels* (blog), http://projecttimetravels.com/how-to-go-back-in-time/.

Tachyons are particles that travel faster than light and could allow one to reach one's destination before one has even left! But science has yet to confirm their existence, and they remain hypothetical.

'Tachyon!' I rolled it around in my mouth. *'Taach-yon.'* The word has a nice sort of feel to it, and it sounds good too, right?

The more I thought about it, armed thus with web page bookmarks and scribbled notes, the more likely it seemed that I had stumbled into a wormhole that summer day in the hills. And that the time crystal that Kubera had given me was a sort of tachyon. Isn't that what Kubera had said when he had handed me the stone? 'I am Digpala, one of the lords of the eight directions, and I shall guide you back. Back to the future! Here is a time crystal . . . Hold on to it tightly when that old lady Dhumavati pushes you into the time-serpent's entrails.' Yes, that must have been it.

The Net gives one access to all sorts of information, but not all of it is first-hand surely. I even looked up and located an answer to 'OK, WTF is a time crystal?', but it was nothing very enlightening, I must say. Rather, I think I can tell them a thing or two about time crystals. If they ever asked me, that is.

For now, I have traded my plans of underwater diving and giving exclusive interviews on leaping across time for studying physics. That's how I'll unveil the mysteries of time and space. I told Karuna of this and she was supportive as ever. She even let out an excited whoop.

'You can do it, CP!' she said. 'Yes, you can! And we will travel together, you and I, through time!'

Sat Tal Again

So there we were, in Sat Tal again. Just the parents, Karuna and me. Mum and Papa are thinking of buying a cottage in the area. We drove around in his new SUV, then hiked up the last leg. Finally, we stopped by a clearing in the woods for a sort of lazy picnic, bringing out the sandwiches my mother made and a date-and-walnut cake from The Sakley's in Nainital.

It wasn't really the most relaxing picnic. Well, there were ants and earthworms and all sorts of critters around. I got stung by a bee that I couldn't even spot when I looked around for it. My mother, though, promptly brought out a tiny tube of toothpaste from her bag and smeared a bit on the swollen bite. The sting started to feel better almost immediately. But what was Ma doing with a tube of toothpaste in her handbag? Then again, I suppose that's what mothers are all about.

After snacking, we were strolling around when we saw this temple. My heart skipped a

beat as I read the sign outside. A sort of arched gate announced 'Om Shri Vana Devi Ma Hidimbi Mandir'. An old man with a knowing look on his wrinkled face greeted us. 'Welcome to Ma Hidimbi's dwelling,' he said. He looked familiar, somehow, though I was sure I had never seen him before.

My parents began asking him about the place.

'This is the temple of the great forest goddess, Ma Hidimbi, wife of Bhima. Bhimtal Lake nearby marks his travels to these parts. And his first, his oldest, most senior wife, Ma Hidimbi, mother of the mighty Ghatotkacha, lived here, ruling the forest and its creatures,' he offered.

The hair on my arms was standing on end. A cold shiver travelled down my spine. That strange time in my life had still not faded away. The past remained here in the present, under the same bright sky. This was *her* land, this was where she continued to live in some other dimension of time. Perhaps I would visit her again, and Ghatotkacha, or perhaps they would come visit me.

That evening, I sat by the hillside and watched the sunset colour the sky orange. Then the earth went dark, and, one by one, the stars appeared. The crooked dip of the Great Bear, the irregular rectangle formed by Sirius. The twinkly pinheads of the Pleiades. They all glittered in the night sky, but not with the fierce magnificence I had known them to, in those days in the forest with Ghatotkacha.

My phone rang, it was my mother.

'Where are you, beta?' she asked, trying to hide the anxiety in her voice.

'I'm just getting back,' I muttered before hanging up. By the white light of the phone, I glimpsed something slither by around the rock on which I was seated.

It was a snake. But I was not afraid. I had learnt the secrets of the forest from my friend Ghatotkacha. The serpent would not hurt me.

I lingered a little longer, and I'm glad I did. A shooting star sped past in the dark sky, and then another. Two wishes. What was it I wanted from the universe now?

To know, the thought came to my mind, *to know and to remember all that I have learnt. And to have the courage to trust nature, and this life.*

These stars carried the secrets of time in them. This same Milky Way, the Aakash Ganga, had watched over me when I was lost in time. And I was still surrounded by those beams from billions of light years away, by ancient galaxies and collapsing, whizzing stars. Suddenly, I remembered a song my mother used to sing a long, long time ago. It was by the Beatles, maybe, about a fool on a hill who saw the world spinning round. I tried to hum it to myself, but I'm not the best singer in the world.

It struck me that, left to ourselves, we get stuck in a different sort of time. In the traps of the present. We forget that things look different from a distance, that yesterday and tomorrow can change the way we look at today. And yet, that today, the now, is all that we have, really. And all our todays become tomorrows and the future beckons; all the challenges we set for ourselves, all our fears and hopes await us. And just like that, I remembered my immediate one.

The upcoming state-level tournament! How had I been ignoring it all these weeks? I got a funny feeling in the pit of my stomach because, after so long, I cherished the idea of being in the present and wanted so badly to prove myself in the now. I was determined to be selected in the team. Yes, I would do everything to play the game, to fight, to win.

My phone rang again. 'Beta, *where* are you?'

'On my way home,' I replied brightly. I could still see the stars smiling at me. I was home already.

The Game

It was the morning of *the* day. The day of the state-level football final qualifier. After countless hours of training, I, Chintamani Dev Gupta, aka Chintu Pintu, woke up feeling like I had indeed made it, joined the big boys in the game. It had taken months of hard work, blood, sweat and tears, for our team to get to the final round. We were up against the fearsome guys from India Public School, with their south Delhi swagger. They were going to be tough competition for sure, what with their midfielder being considered one of the best in the league. As the school's goalkeeper, I felt a special sense of responsibility to the team, to the game, to myself.

But I was ready. I was not going to let Bhaichung Bhutia down—not today, of all days. As I gulped down the cold coffee my mother had so lovingly prepared for me, I thought of all the pesky 'if only's. If only Karuna could have been here today. If only—though it was utterly impossible—Ghatotkacha could have travelled across time to cheer me on . . .

But the bus was honking already and I was rudely transported back to reality. Just thinking about Ghatto had given me the rush of strength I needed. As I grabbed my bag, my mother flashed me an encouraging smile and my father pulled me into a tight hug. 'You can do it, Chintamani!' he said.

I had a lot worth fighting for. I would do it—yes, I would!

The atmosphere in the locker room was as intense as that on a battlefield. Boys and more boys everywhere, changing into their jerseys, donning their equipment and padding—what else but modern-day weaponry and armour. The smell of anticipation hanging in the air.

Minutes later, Mr Subramanian strode in, a Manchester United cap on his big bald head, a whistle in one hand, a clipboard in another. I groaned internally (I'm so not a Manchester fanboy—they are far too overrated!). He did a quick scan of the room before going back out. As he called out the line-up, the boys huddled together by the pitch and cheered. We were greeted by loud screams and whistles from an excited audience. I spotted my parents, their eyes gleaming with pride, wide smiles spread across their faces, animatedly waving a banner held up high above them. It gave me a warm feeling to see them together in a crowd, once again in love and safe in each other's arms. And there beside them was . . . Karuna! Yes, there she was—watching intently as she waited for the game to begin. Her gaze met mine in an electric moment and my stomach lurched when she waved at me.

My eyes then travelled to our school's cheerleaders brandishing streamers and pom-poms, the biggest grins ever on their bright faces. Even though they had been forbidden by our principal from wearing short skirts and were in salwar-kameez suits, that clearly hadn't dimmed their excitement one bit. When the teams ran on to the field, they squealed and the stands roared.

As the twenty-two players faced each other and shook hands before the kick-off, I could have sworn the IPS team's striker in front of me gave me a death stare. I looked away coolly, instead watching the referee, a tall man with unnaturally huge biceps, come forward for the toss. The coin was flipped and both teams were stationed by the captains in their positions. It was now or never. I had been anticipating this moment for such a long time.

I could feel the tension balled up in my stomach, coursing down my arms, in every muscle of my body. Then I heard the piercing whistle. *We* will *win this fight*, I told myself. And I was in action, powerfully flitting from side to side to guard my post.

The first half of the game was uneventful, neither team having been able to score. A substitute on the IPS team, who was called in after half-time, ended up playing way better than the key player and made us rather anxious. A few free kicks that went wide and some throw-ins later, the score still remained unchanged. The match had now come down to its last ten minutes. With neither team having a goal on the scoreboard, it was still anyone's game. We just *had* to find a way to break the deadlock.

To top that, the IPS striker had come way too close to scoring a few goals in the second half, and I could almost feel the pressure weighing me down like a millstone. Five minutes on the clock and he was going for it yet again. The crowd erupted wildly over the striker as he slowly made his way across the field, skilfully dribbling past our agitated defenders almost halfway from the centre line. *Uh-oh*, my mates were struggling—I knew it was time to brace myself. Now it was up to me. Very slowly, I bent my knees and locked my hands close to each other, my shin guards digging into my skin. My ears were ringing with the roars of exhilaration and anticipation from the audience.

In an unhindered moment, almost at the edge of the penalty box, my opponent bent backward ever so slightly and, with a powerful instep kick, shot the ball to the left. I just couldn't gauge where it was headed for half a second, as it burst from a jumble of stomping feet. Would it swing out and miss the bar? *No! It might just make it!* Simultaneously I dived to the side, my hands outstretched desperately.

The microseconds slowed down, the past, the present and the future all coming together as I soared towards the hurtling ball. I stretched every muscle of my body and steeled every nerve, until I was slicing through the air like a bird, a bee, a butterfly.

Like a boy who had flown through the air before. I could feel someone, something, lifting me higher and higher until the tip of my middle finger kissed tough leather and I became one with the goal. I *was* the goal.

We won.

Later, when everybody in the team hugged and congratulated me, I thought about my save more deeply. A minute after what was soon dubbed 'the deadly deflection' and 'the season's most incredible clearance', Mohan, our opportunist striker, had scored the winning goal—a chip shot. A Messi classic. It truly was a spectacular victory.

But I wondered if I had done it all by myself. I couldn't see Ghatotkacha with me on that football field, but maybe he had been there?

Or maybe he hadn't. Ghatotkacha was a part of me, as I was a part of him. He had shared his strength, his courage, his friendship and his magic. And I, in that moment, in my own twenty-first century way, had become him. Truly, life was a game. There would be more games to play, more challenges to come. But he had taught me well, and I—we—would face them.

As I went out to search for Karuna amidst the sea of excited faces, I found that I was whistling the same long, warbling whistle I had taught him, during what were among the best days of my life. As the days to come promised to be.

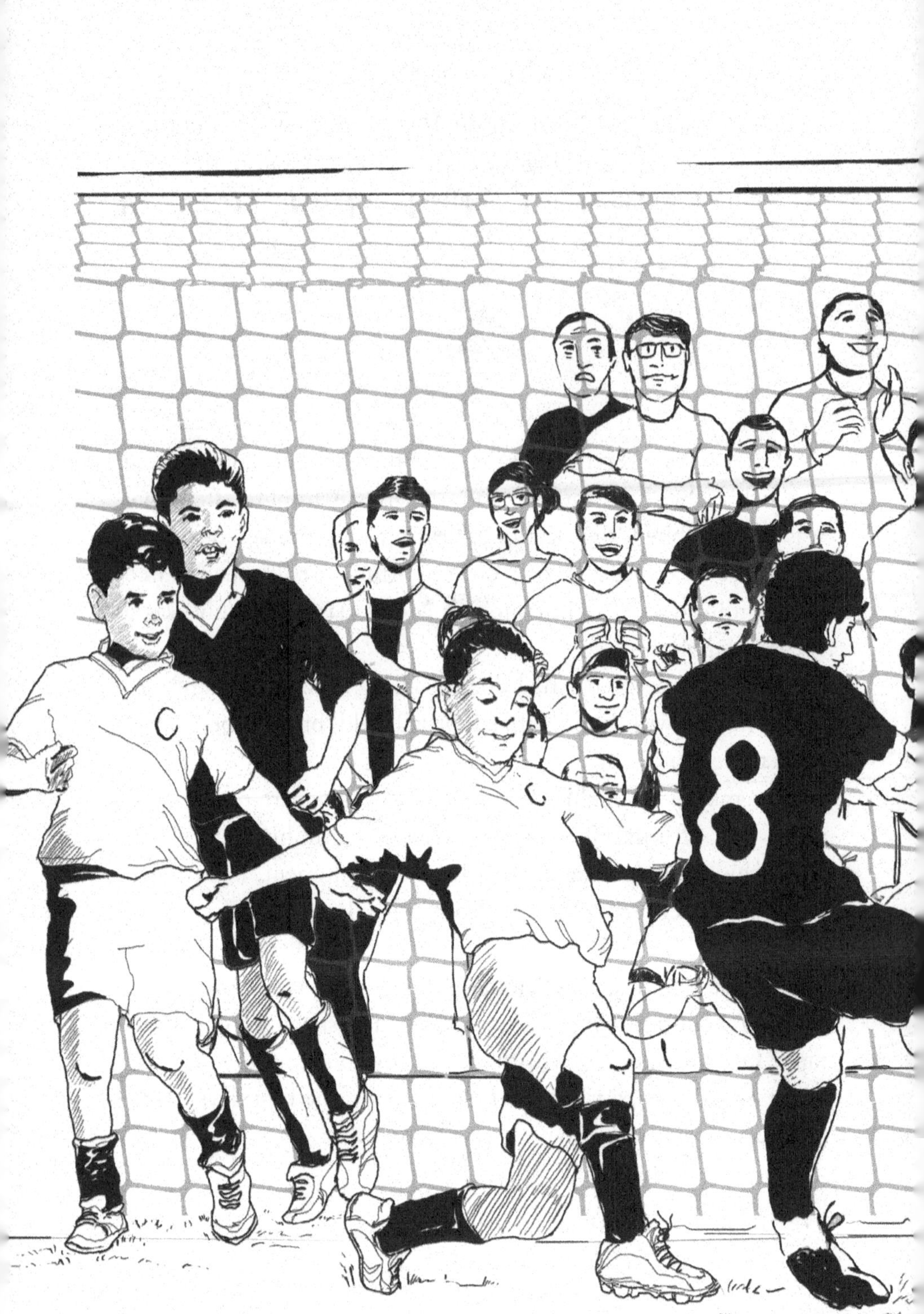

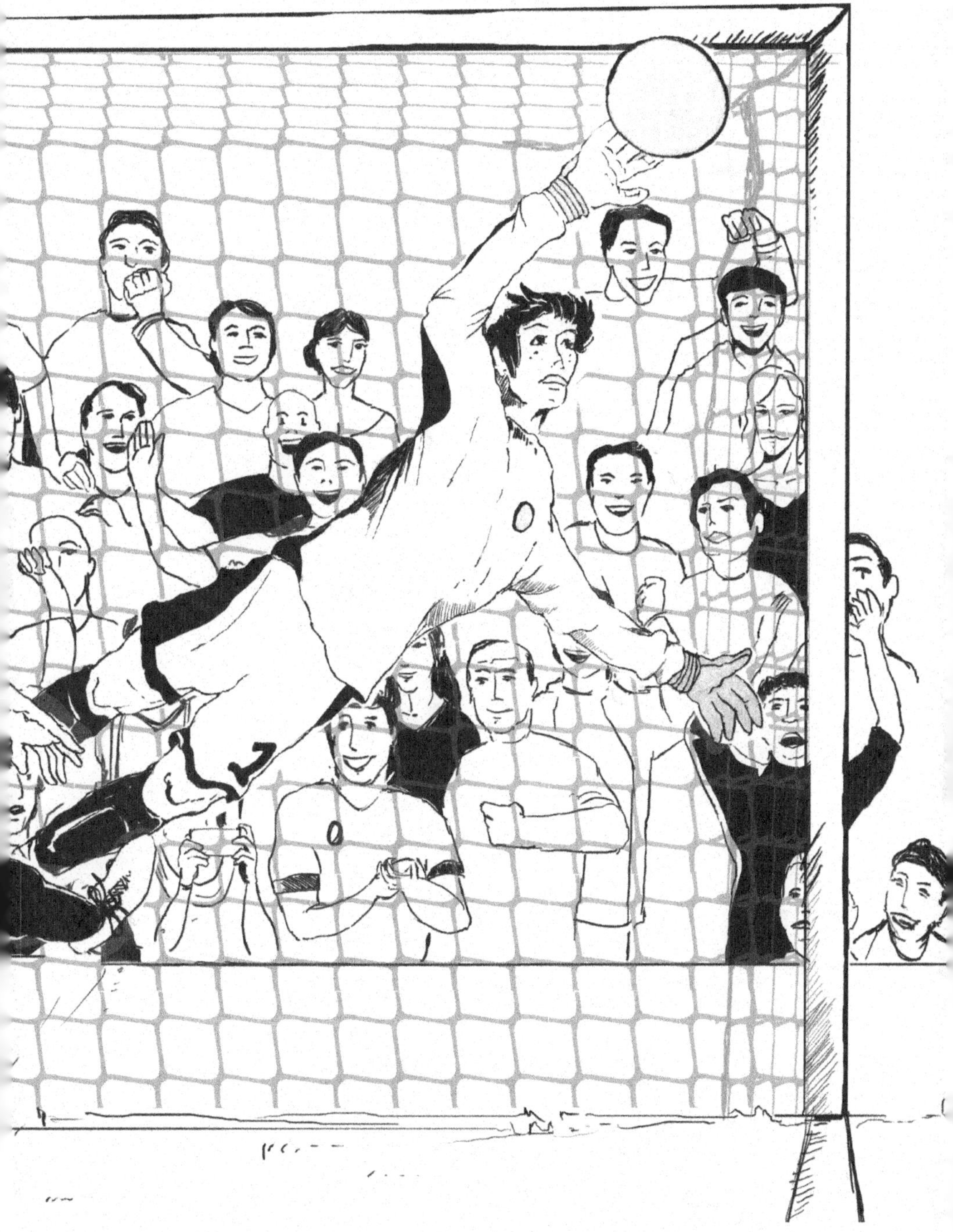

Acknowledgements

My thanks to Hemali Sodhi, Sohini Mitra, Kankana Basu and all at Puffin and PRH India for believing in the book. To Anisha Lalvani for her constant and thoughtful support. To Jaidev Pant for a fresh perspective and editing inputs. To Ujan Dutta for the illustrations, to Neelima P Aryan and Gunjan Ahlawat for such a distinct visual identity.

To the magical writing time at The Taj Gateway Resort in Corbett Park and at the beautiful Alila Fort Bishangarh. Thank you for giving me silence and nature and nurture.